PEACH PIT

SIXTEEN STORIES OF UNSAVORY WOMEN

EDITED BY

MOLLY LLEWELLYN AND KRISTEL BUCKLEY

DZANC BOOKS

DZANC BOOKS

2580 Craig Rd.
Ann Arbor, MI 48103
www.dzancbooks.org

Library of Congress Cataloging-in-Publication Data Available Upon Request

First US edition: September 2023
ISBN 9781950539871
Interior design by Michelle Dotter
Cover design by Matthew Revert
Artwork by Megan Ellen Macdonald

"Caller" by K-Ming Chang, originally published in *Soft Punk Magazine*, 2021
"Amaranth" by Lauren Groff, originally published in *Lucky Peach*, 2013
"Maps" by Vanessa Chan, originally published in *Joyland Magazine*, 2021
"The Monolith" by Chaya Bhuvaneswar, originally published in *Narrative Magazine*, 2017

Printed in the United States of America

10   9   8   7   6   5   4   3   2   1

CONTENTS

Who has not asked himself at some time or other: am I a monster or is this what it means to be a person?

—Clarice Lispector

Peach pits are poisonous. This is not a mistake. Girlhood is growing fruit around cyanide. It will never be yours for swallowing.

—Brenna Twohy

EDITORS' NOTE

A PERSON WHO IS morally gray is described to be someone who "cannot be described as wholly good nor wholly evil." They are someone who does bad things for good reasons, or good things for bad ones. They are human.

Historically, women in literature have fallen into tropes. The number of these differs, but will always feature the virgin, the whore, the mother, and the old maid. A good woman moves from virgin to mother and a bad one from whore to old maid. There is no term given for a woman in the middle, therefore no room for a woman to exist outside of these definitions. A woman who doesn't fit these classifications doesn't exist. If she falls within the grey space, she doesn't. She is a corrupted angel and someone else is to blame, or she must be doing good things with nefarious intentions. That is the way it has always been, both in life and in prose.

In a time where society is increasingly divisive, social media, echo chambers, and our bias toward positive reinforcement is making it hard to listen. People are becoming their stereotypes, and we're forming teams or camps, aligning ourselves with extremes. We're losing empathy for those who do not look or speak like us or believe what we do. Surrounded by these binaries, it is more important than ever to pay attention to the grey space. Because that is the space where we are all the same. It's where we make bad decisions, we fail, we fall, and we hope that nobody sees it.

As human beings, we are not a sum of our parts. White men have an abundance of literature to illustrate this, but the rest of us simply have not been represented to the same extent.

Nowhere is this more apparent than with the women found in the margins of society. Trans women and women of color for far too long have had to squeeze into the tiny space made for them. So often in literature, these women are only heard when the topic is something they can uniquely understand. They are brought into the conversation to talk about the trauma and tragedy that their identity and history has contributed to, but their joy, love, fears, and anxieties are ignored if it is not tied to their difference. No person is only what they present, and though our identities often shape our perspectives, these women of color have so much more to tell the world than simply I'm not white.

When putting together this collection, we wanted to make sure we gave space to marginalized authors, particularly women of color, to create these unlikeable, messy protagonists.

As much as society tries to repress it, there is a little darkness inside all of us. We have not been allowed the space to make mistakes, to be messy and angry and imperfect and vulgar—to lean into the ways it shapes us and informs our decision-making. Throughout this anthology, we wanted to feature female characters that muddy the idea what is "acceptable." These stories look at what it means to be a woman who toes the line between "right" and "wrong"—one who not only occupies this morally grey space, but fully embraces it. The women in Peach Pit get inside our heads and live out on the page what we can't do or wouldn't dare to. Some will satisfy us, knowing that at least somewhere there was justice. Others will teach us about what it means to be a different type of woman, one who walks and competes with not only the expectations her femininity dictates, but those of her race and/or sexuality.

In these pages, you'll see women at their most unlikeable. Reading about them makes us uncomfortable because we can't always agree with them, or because sometimes we secretly do. The decisions that they make aren't always correct, or justifiable, but they are honest.

A person who is morally gray is described as someone who is not wholly good or wholly evil. For too long, to be a woman in fiction is to have made the choice. We hope to remedy this.

FUCKBOY MUSEUM

DEESHA PHILYAW

I'm gettin' tired of yo' shit...
— e. badu

Welcome to the Fuckboy Museum
a repository of reckoning

Come inside. Chill.

TONIGHT, I'M MAKING LINGUINE with white clam sauce, my favorite dish. I make it with loads of garlic, the way Mama likes it. I get the clams fresh from the fish market and shuck them myself. I cook every day and as often as I can with fresh fish, herbs, vegetables, and farm-fresh meats. Cooking seems to be a selling point with men on dating apps. They wax nostalgic about how their grandmama made their granddaddy three square meals a day, seven days a week, while working and keeping the house clean and raising kids and overlooking their granddaddy's outside kids, and how she never complained. Most likely, their grandmamas stayed for purely economic reasons. Back then, divorce was an express train to poverty for women, especially Black women. These men don't talk about the times their sweet Nana went upside Pop Pop's head with the same cast-iron skillet she made his cornbread in. And in fairness, maybe they don't know. Sometimes women don't pass their stories down to their sons. And sometimes they do, but the sons don't listen. After all, women aren't for listening to.

Shawn (b. 1971)
Coffee, 2016
Abridged transcript of conversation at Starbuck's

Shawn: So you're a writer. Anything I might've heard of?

Lilli: Yes, I've written several award-winning, *New York Times* bestselling books—

Shawn: Huh. People tell me all the time that I should write a book.

Lilli: Oh?

Shawn: Yeah. *(typing on his phone)* Sent you a link to my blog. Let me know what you think.

Lilli: *(opens the link on her phone, notes date of most recent blog post: July 23, 2008)*

"Ms. Williams, what do you do for a living?" The detective sips the peppermint tea I served, then returns the cup to its saucer.

"I write urban horror for children," I say. "Remember those *Scary Stories to Tell in the Dark* series we used to read in the eighties?"

"I do."

"Well, instead of detached body parts and dark woods, my stories feature neighborhood watch patrols that only watch the Black people in the neighborhood, bogus CYS investigations resulting in indefinite stays with white foster mothers who just 'love' their wards' 'untamed curls' (*Miss Anne's House*), and beloved fathers held at gunpoint by racist cops during routine traffic stops (*Daddy's Not Home*). No offense."

"None taken."

"*Scary Tales You Hope Don't Come True* started as a popular anonymous blog series and became a popular book series after a tenacious agent convinced me to pitch the first collection to all the big publishing houses. A bidding war ensued, and the collection debuted on the *New York Times* bestseller list under my pseudonym, L.R. Stewart. But I kept my day job here at Kimbilio because Mama needed the help."

The detective scribbles in her notebook. "Your mother lives here with you?"

"She would say I live here with her." I chuckle. "And I suppose she's right. My father inherited this property from his father, and he and Mama turned it into a B&B, Kimbilio Bed & Breakfast. Shortly after I was born, they added the restaurant and built a cottage out back for the three of us to live in. My father passed away the day before my twenty-first birthday."

"I'm sorry for your loss."

"Thank you. Since then, I've seen the world, but never wanted to make anywhere else home. Not even when I got married. I got married right here in this parlor. Memories of my father are in these rooms and in the gardens out back that I helped him plant as a child. My memories of his care and protection are in this place."

Robert (b. 1971)

[redacted], 2017

Match.com private message transcript

Robert: Hey

Lilli: Hey

Robert: [image of an erect, unimpressive penis]

"Kimbilio" means "safe haven" in Kiswahili, and that's what our B&B is. A home away from home for our guests, as it was for our staff, who were like family. We all cried when I made the difficult decision to let them go. In addition to a generous severance, I insisted the staff take whatever they wanted from the walk-in meat freezer. When we said goodbye to our last guest, the only thing that remained was a box of ribeye steaks.

◦❦◦

The detective crosses her legs and leans forward. If she's trying to hide her curves in that plain black pantsuit, it's not working. "So you're a writer, and you run this place?" she asks.

"Just the inn now. Mama had a stroke last year which left her partially blind and paralyzed," I say. "I couldn't manage everything, on top of being her caretaker. So I closed the restaurant. We live on my book advances and royalties, with a bit of income from occasional B&B guests."

"And you said you're married? Your husband lives here too?"

"Not anymore. Oscar, my ex, used to help Mama and me run the B&B. But we're divorced now."

∽❧⌢

I can't say I miss Oscar. Truth was, the older he got, the more he was just…there. There like the big oak check-in desk was there. Sturdy, useful, familiar. Meanwhile, the older *I* got, the more I felt luscious and wild and new every day. And it wasn't just me I wanted to explore. In the last decade of our marriage, I traveled to twenty-six countries. Oscar chose to stay at home and watch TV. He wouldn't even go to the movies with me. And he refused to go to marriage counseling.

"It's like someone shut off the lights inside him," I told my best friend Talibah.

After he reluctantly signed the divorce papers, I had to ask him to leave Kimbilio. He'd moved into one of the guestrooms, proposed that we be housemates, and even offered to pay double the market rate for rent. And out of pity, I almost let him. But Talibah reminded me that the next chapter of my life couldn't begin until he left.

Alexander (b. 1970)

Beef Wellington, 2018

Text message transcript

MON, OCT 29, 2018 9:02 AM

Alexander: Good morning beautiful

Lilli: Good morning

Alexander: wyd

Lilli: Eating breakfast. How are you?

THU, NOV 1, 2018 10:10 AM

Alexander: Good morning beautiful

Lilli: Hi.

Alexander: wyd

Lilli: Just finished breakfast.

TUE, NOV 6, 2018 12:39 PM

Alexander: Good morning beautiful

Lilli: Actually, it's the afternoon.

Alexander: Oh my bad. Hru?

Lilli: I'm fine. How are you?

WED, NOV 7, 2018 8:39 AM

Alexander: Good morning beautiful

Lilli: Hey. Do you want to meet for coffee or something?

WED, NOV 7, 2018 4:53 PM

Alexander: wyd

Lilli: Wondering if you're going to reply to my last msg

Alexander: Yeah coffee is good

WED, NOV 7, 2018 6:01 PM

Lilli: Hey. Tomorrow afternoon? Or Friday morning?

Alexander: Ok

Lilli: Which one?

> **MON, NOV 12, 2018 11:22 AM**
>
> Alexander: Good morning beautiful. Yr profile sez u like 2 cook. U shld make me some Beef Wellington.

Mama says I'm reaping what I've sown for, quote, *throwing away a good man.* "You broke poor Oscar's heart, and now your heart is broken," she told me once, back when I used to tell her about my dating disasters.

"I don't let these men anywhere near my heart. And what made Oscar *good*, Mama? The fact that he didn't beat me? Or that he was breathing and not six feet under?"

Mama clutched her heart with her right hand, the one that isn't paralyzed.

Yeah, it was a shitty thing to say, but Mama's wrong to expect me to settle.

∽✑∽

"Ms. Williams?"

"Oh! Sorry. Just got lost in thought for a minute."

The detective runs her palm over her low-cut fade. "I asked if you're currently dating anyone?"

> **MansaMusa99** (b. 1972)
>
> *Pride Goeth,* 2019
>
> *Tinder dating app profile*
>
> In lieu of a personal photo, there is an image of a lion. He is yellow-white with flames. He is made

> of fire. The two-part caption reads: DONT [sic]
> MISTAKE MY KINDNESS FOR WEAKNESS
> (above the lion) and THE BEAST IN ME IS
> SLEEPING, NOT DEAD (below the lion)

"It's so lovely when their profile includes an indirect threat," Talibah said. It was Valentine's Day 2019, the third one after I divorced Oscar, and we were scrolling through dating app profiles, sipping Prosecco and eating grilled fig, ham, and brie sandwiches I'd made for us. We toasted to being each other's Valentine and to the release of my tenth book in the *Scary Tales…* series, *Tales of a Fifth-Grade Plantation Field Trip.*

At that point, Talibah had been on the dating apps for about five years longer than I had, but we were equally jaded about our prospects.

"I only attract filthy Ques —" I said.

"That's redundant."

"—and Sigmas."

"Sigmas are basically Ques who do extra community service."

"Listen to this one," I said. "'I am looking for someone loyal, who cooks and values family. Marital status: Tell You Later.' Translation: My wife of twenty-five years cheated and she's divorcing me because of course I won't file and I can't bear to be alone and I haven't even moved out yet but I'm looking for someone new to disappoint, rather than looking inward."

"You're like a fuckboy whisperer," Talibah said.

"'Must appreciate old school principals.'" I laughed and showed Talibah my phone. "I appreciate Mr. McCormick from Carson Elementary School! Remember him?"

"You're drunk."

"Maybe! I'm sure old-school principles include holding doors for the ladies and being the head of the household. But wait! There's more! 'Women these days don't appreciate a Real Man. I can understand why some of you are single and unclaimed.'"

"Like, what are we? Luggage?"

Given Talibah's paltry experiences, I had embarked upon post-divorce dating the way one embarks upon recreational gold mining. But within a year, I too had abandoned the fantasy of finding the kind of loving life partners our mothers had. Talibah and I went on speed dates that led nowhere fast. The guys who were cheating on their wives and girlfriends? We became experts at ferreting them out. The ones who, if a woman says she's a surgeon, interrupt to talk about the first-aid kit they have at home? Those guys? Blocked. Dudes who just wanted friends with benefits, we were fine with that too. All we asked is that they be emotionally stable, intelligent, respectful, healthy, consistent, and able to afford to go out from time to time. Instead, we got stood up and ghosted.

But Talibah and I agreed that the most egregious were men who simply wanted to be entertained by bright, attractive, funny women. Men who couldn't hold a basic conversation to save their lives and were allergic to making plans. "But will text you into oblivion, if you let them," Talibah says. "So now I block them as soon as it's clear they're not going to make an effort."

BriDawn (b. unknown)

Breadcrumbing

urbandictionary.com entries

"The act of sending out flirtatious, but noncommittal text messages (i.e. "breadcrumbs") . . . in order to lure a sexual partner without expending much effort."

> "When a person flirts here or there through DM/
> texts, just to keep the other person interested. They
> have no intention of taking things further, but they
> like the attention."

At forty-five, after a lifetime of weed abstinence, I started getting high like everyone else. The first time was to celebrate my
divorce being finalized. Talibah and I jetted off to a 420-friendly
resort in Belize. The first night, she shotgunned me on the beach,
then turned on some Tanerélle. I could taste the bass in my mouth,
metallic and smooth. I danced toward the water and back. I swayed
and flipped Talibah off when she hooted at my "white girl" moves,
and I bodyrolled. I imagined dirty dancing with Everett, a good-
looking broadcast engineer at a local TV station. I'd matched with
him right after a six-month hiatus from the dating apps. Everett
shared, via in-app messaging, that he'd lost both his parents to cancer in the last year. Because he'd been vulnerable, I thought I could
be too. We talked about grief, and I told him about my daddy's
death and how post-divorce dating had been tough and how I'd
started to become a bit disillusioned. In the messaging interface,
I saw three dots (which meant he was typing) for what felt like an
eternity. Finally: "The Disillusioned need not apply." And then he
blocked me.

I twirled away from imaginary Everett, dug my toes into the
sand, and wrapped my arms around my body.

It's a miracle I didn't start hunting sooner.

∽◉∼

"No," I tell the detective. "I'm not seeing anyone at the moment."

> **Terrance** (b. 1971)
>
> *Ghost Story: I,* 2022
>
> Text message transcript
>
> ### SUN, JAN 9, 12:32 AM
>
> Terrance: I had a wonderful evening.
>
> Lilli: Me too. I haven't laughed that hard in forever. Thank you!
>
> Terrance: Your laughter is like music. I think it's my new favorite sound…
>
> Lilli: High praise coming from a musician!
>
> Terrance: Date #3, it's the magic number
>
> Lilli: #SchoolhouseRock…Nice.
>
> Terrance: #GenXShit
>
> Terrance: Good night, beautiful
>
> Lilli: Good night, handsome

The last man I cooked for claimed his mama named him Be, and of course he had locs and smelled like sandalwood. He was tall and beautiful with a thinning hairline, which made it hard to gauge his age. He could've been a young-looking fifty, or a prematurely balding thirty-five. I couldn't call it. Be's old school R&B/soul/funk cover band, The Both Ands, was the house band at my favorite dive bar. Be sang on occasion, but mostly he played guitar with his back to the audience. He swore he wasn't trying to be like Miles.

When I walk in the door at Lucy's High Dive, Joe, the owner, always has a margarita waiting for me. By the time The Both Ands come on, I'm buzzed, full of tequila, hot wings and Cajun fries.

Buzzed isn't enough to get me out on the dance floor, a generous description of the cleared space in front of the band, near the entrance. For me to dance, there has to be some Cameo or Rick James or Cheryl Lynn. Maybe The Gap Band.

The night I met Be, it was Cameo's "Candy" that got me off the stool. I danced with far more enthusiasm than skill. I leaned forward shoulder first and wound my backside slowly against an invisible partner. I tossed my head back, closed my eyes, and shimmied. When I opened my eyes again, I found Be staring at me, no longer playing with his back to the room. His look said he was playing for me, and only me. I stared back and danced my awkward-but-exuberant Black girl dance for him.

At the end of the set, he joined me at the bar and introduced himself. "I'm Be, spelled *B-e*."

"Of course you are."

"Excuse me?" He laughed. I detected a lilt when he spoke and imagined his very accomplished West Indian mother somewhere disappointed in his life choices.

I extended my hand. "I'm Lilli." We shook.

"Indeed, you are a lovely flower. What are you drinking?"

I waved away the compliment, but accepted another margarita. Be said he couldn't help but notice me dancing, and I wasn't sure if that was a compliment or not.

"I'm always in here dancing," I said. "What's so special about tonight?"

Be shrugged and downed one of the glasses of water Joe had set in front of us, along with a basket of fries, on the house.

"Whenever Kerry introduced the guys in the band, I thought he was saying "B," like the letter. Is 'Be' short for something?"

"Nope. Nothing about me is short."

I smirked. "Nice." I polished off my margarita and signaled Joe for another one.

Be munched on the fries and slid one into my mouth. "So…"
I said, between bites. "I was reading the other day about how, years
ago, a reporter asked Eric Clapton how it felt to be the greatest living
guitarist. And Clapton says, 'I don't know. You'd have to ask Prince.'
Of course, this was before Prince left us."

"Well, gorgeous, I hate to break it to you, but that story is apocryphal."

"Nooooo. Dammit. That was my go-to story when I talk to musicians so I can sound like I know what the fuck I'm talking about."

"Yeah? How often you talk to musicians?"

"Often enough." I licked the salt on the rim of my new drink, tried
to look casual, tried not to think about the last musician I'd talked to.

"Listen," Be said, leaning in, "my break is almost over and I still
need to take a piss, so I hope you'll forgive my cutting to chase: come
home with me tonight."

"How old are you?"

"Okay, that's…not a response I was expecting."

"What were you expecting?"

"Either 'yes' or 'fuck yes.'"

"Fuck no."

"Why not?"

"Because, if we're cutting to the chase, I don't know where your
dick has been."

"There are so many ways I would fuck you. Many of them don't
require my dick."

The band started warming up. I sighed. My pussy did jump when
Be said "apocryphal." Maybe he was different. Maybe I wouldn't end
up hunting him.

Then, as Be leaned toward me, smiling, I noticed it. Not much
bigger than a speck, really, but undeniable: a black spot on his incisor
at the gum line. A rotting tooth.

I sucked on the lime wedge from my drink and then dropped it in the glass. I looked up from Be's mouth to his eyes and asked, "Are you going to be the next terrible thing that happens to me?"

Alexander (b. 1969)

Bet, 2018-2022

Text message transcript

MON, NOV 12, 2018 11:22 AM

Alexander: Good morning beautiful. Yr profile sez u like 2 cook. U shld make me some Beef Wellington.

TUE, NOV 20, 2018 3:18 PM

Alexander: wyd

THU, NOV 22, 2018 11:55 AM

Alexander: Happy Thanksgiving

TUE, DEC 25, 2018 3:18 PM

Alexander: Merry Christmas! What you get me???

TUE, JAN 1, 2019 2:48 PM

Alexander: Happy New Year!

FRI, FEB 1, 2019 9:13 AM

Alexander: Happy Black History Month

FRI, JAN 1, 2021 1:27 PM

Alexander: Happy New Year!

> **SAT, JAN 1, 1:27 PM**
>
> Alexander: Happy New Year!
>
> **SAT, FEB 5, 2:06 AM**
>
> Lilli: Still want that Beef Wellington? No need to make plans. Whenever you show up is fine. I'll drop whatever I'm doing and cook.
>
> **SAT, FEB 5, 2:08 AM**
>
> Alexander: Word? Bet. U cool as hell.

The first time wasn't a hunt. It was an accident. Like Talibah, I would block guys. And when scrolling the apps started to feel like a full-time job, when the rollercoaster of emotions from hour to hour or day to day left me dull-eyed and without an appetite, I took breaks for weeks, months at a time. But something—loneliness, horniness, optimism, masochism—always brought me back.

> **Cedric** (b. 1974)
>
> *Supercalifragilisticexpialidocious,* 2017
>
> *Tinder dating app private message transcript*
>
> Cedric: You look like you use a lot of big words.

I had just emailed my editor the draft of my sixteenth book, *Akilah and the No-Knock Warrant,* when Alexander showed up. True to my word, I skipped my mani-pedi appointment and we went to the grocery store. I planned to feed him, fuck him, send him home, and never see him again.

I cooked, we ate. Alexander was exactly who he had been in his text messages, so conversation consisted mostly of him marveling that I'd actually cooked for him, that I'm actually a good cook, and that I actually own this "big-ass crib." He wanted to take pictures of the Beef Wellington to post on Instagram, but he'd forgotten his phone in his car. I took a picture and told him I'd text it to him.

After some vigorous couch-fucking, I loaded the dishwasher and packed up leftovers for Alexander. He sidled up behind me and tried to kiss my neck. I scooted out of reach and told him I had something else for him to take home. He followed me through the kitchen to the meat freezer. That lonely box of ribeyes would be a consolation prize for him, and the true end of another chapter for me: No more dating apps.

I don't know where the spark of mischief came from, but I bolted from the freezer and locked it behind me with Alexander inside. Figured I'd scare him a bit.

He yelled and pounded on the door a few times and then stopped. The silence that followed haunts me more than his calling my name.

Alexander's body blocked the door, but I could open it just enough to slide inside. I didn't want to touch him, but I didn't have to. His unblinking stare at the ceiling confirmed he was gone. Maybe because he texted like a tween, I didn't consider the possibility that his fifty-three-year-old heart couldn't take my shenanigans.

Alexander (1969-2022)

Last Supper, 2022

Text message transcript

SAT, FEB 19 1:33 PM

Alexander: Wuts yr address?

SAT, FEB 19 1:45 PM

Lilli: 546 Hillcrest

SAT, MARCH 5 3:33 PM

Alexander: omw

SAT, MARCH 5 9:03 PM

Lilli: What the hell??? Did you have to *build* a
car before you could drive over? I'm
turning in. Good night!

Lilli: Oh and here's what you missed out on...

[image of a bomb-ass Beef Wellington]

Guilt is so...pedestrian.

ༀ

This year, I resolved to luxuriate in simplicity. I treat myself to
bamboo sheets for my bed, soy candles, luminescent bath salts, and
more vinyl for my collection. The physical act of playing a record,
being still, and listening to it from start to finish is so satisfying, like
reading a good book in one sitting.

I walk over to the record player, a Victrola Empire, and put on
some Nina Simone while the detective pages through her notebook.

"Nina speaks the truth," I say. "We have to get up from the table
when love's no longer being served."

"Ms. Williams, when was the last time you saw Terrance
Hutchinson?"

Terrance (b. 1971)

Ghost Story: II, 2022

Text message transcript

FRI, JAN 14, 11:59 PM

Terrance: What were those cheese pastry puff things we had tonight called again? I didn't catch what the waiter said.

Lilli: The amuse-bouche? Gougères.

Terrance: Gougères! Thank you. Well, my bouche was amused. And your bouche was tasty too…

Lilli: Mmmm. You're a great kisser

Terrance: And your mouth is absolutely sinful

Lilli: Oh my… *sigh* I'm having serious vorfreude right now.

Terrance: Is that German for "regret that I didn't spend the night with Terrance"?

Lilli: Ha! It's "the joyful, intense anticipation that comes from imagining future pleasures."

Terrance: It's like I'm dating a sexy dictionary lol

Lilli: LMAO!

Lilli: Can't wait to see you at the rink tomorrow

Terrance: Same. Noon still good for you?

Lilli: Yep! I haven't skated in years, so I'm going to turn in now, rest up. Sweet dreams…

Terrance: They will be, if I dream about you again.

Lilli: Tell me about your dream

Terrance: We did what we would've done tonight, if you had stayed…

Lilli: Funny how the conscious and the subconscious always seem to meet in the crotch lol

Terrance: LOL

Lilli: Tomorrow night, I have someone coming to stay with my mom, so I can stay with you.

Terrance: Sweet!

Lilli: Until then, I'll meet you in dreamland, handsome. Good night.

Terrance: Good night ☐

SAT, JAN 15, 12:05 PM

Lilli: Hey! Did you drive or take a Lyft? Not sure if you're having trouble finding a space. I had to park behind the doughnut shop.

SAT, JAN 15, 12:15 PM

Lilli: We said noon right?

SAT, JAN 15, 12:25 PM

Lilli: Just called you…

SAT, JAN 15, 12:45 PM

Lilli: Are you ok?

SAT, JAN 15, 1:00 PM

Lilli: I'm heading home. Please let me know you're
ok. I'm worried…

SAT, JAN 15, 7:37 PM

Lilli: Saw that hilarious Snoop Dogg meme
you just posted on Facebook. And the pic
of you and your friends tonight at
the beer garden. Good to know
you're not dead…I guess.

SUN, JAN 30, 2:21 AM

Lilli: I haven't had sex in almost three years.
Three years since I've had to feel around
beneath my comforter at the foot of
my bed on laundry day for hastily
discarded panties, each pair a memory,
a quiver. I miss being fucked so good
that I catch myself stretching,
arching my back, purring at the
flashbacks for hours, for days,
afterwards. And I'm scared, terrified
actually, that I'm going to die
without having sex with someone I
actually like, at least one more time.

Lilli: FUCK YOU

> **Author Unknown**
>
> *Trapping Tips: Use the Right Bait for Each Critter*
>
> Source: outdoorlife.com
>
> "The bait has to be something enticing to the animal."

Perhaps *trapping* is more accurate than *hunting*? *Luring the prey to its demise* is a more apt description. Still, after Alexander, the image of myself as a hunter persisted. In prose, the active voice is much more alive than the passive voice. I felt more alive after Alexander. My appetite returned with a vengeance.

Terrance's dinner invitation text arrived wrapped in an apology about a month after Alexander's. I told him I was sorry for cursing at him in my last message. He didn't apologize for standing me up, just said he "had a lot going on at that time" and he couldn't wait to see me again.

Once again, Beef Wellington was on the menu. But before dinner, I asked Terrance to help me get a few things out of the meat freezer. Before he lost consciousness, as he lay bleeding, I asked him if he really thought he deserved a home-cooked meal. Predictably, he called me a bitch.

∽∾∽

"The last time I saw Terrance was a few months ago." I refilled the detective's cup and topped off my own. "He stood me up, and this wasn't the first time. So I texted him and cussed him out and blocked his number."

"And Berkshire Clarke?"

"Who?"

Be (b. unknown)

Not To Be, 2022

Text message transcript

FRI, JUNE 3, 1:14 AM

Be: [eyeballs emoji]

SAT, JUNE 11, 2:55 AM

Be: hey

SUN, JUNE 12, 12:59 AM

Be: hey

TUE, JUNE 14, 4:27 PM

Lilli: Do you want to come over for dinner?
No need to make plans. Whenever you
show up is fine. I'll drop whatever
I'm doing and cook.

"Ms. Williams, is something funny?"

"No. Sorry." I cleared my throat. "It's just that *Berkshire* told me his name was…never mind. He never showed either."

∽☙∼

In the end, Be wasn't a terrible thing that happened to me. I did take him home the night he propositioned me at Lucy's. We had nine minutes of sex before he fell asleep. That should have been the end of it. But when do mediocre men ever go away quietly? At Lucy's, he would come over between sets, steal my fries, and ask, "When can I see you again?" But he never followed through, never made a plan. Every week, it was the same. Like Fuckboy Groundhog Day. *And he kept texting me.*

Lillith Williams (b. 1971)

Fuckboys: A Triptych, 2022

Mixed media: flesh, blood, bones, bullshit

I imagine my museum through Be's eyes, the way he saw it the night he came for dinner. My exhibits fluttering in the wind created when I opened the freezer door. Dozens of artifacts printed on stark white paper hanging from strips of twine stuck to the ceiling with cold-weather tape. Even more lining the shelves and the walls.

As I shut the freezer door behind me, perhaps Be read: *Your mouth is absolutely sinful.*

Or maybe it was: *The Disillusioned need not apply.*

And maybe, just before he turned to face me, he read: *FUCK YOU.*

But I know for a fact that the last thing he saw in this world was the exhibit I held up to his face in my left hand, as I gripped the sledgehammer in my right: *When can I see you again?*

After I removed the tarp covering Terrance and Alexander, I dragged Be over to join them, to be curated.

∾◦∽

The detective tapped her pen on her notebook. She glanced around the parlor and then finally trained her eyes on me.

"Mr. Clarke's car is still parked out front. Alexander Murray's car was found parked three doors down from here. And records show a Lyft dropped Mr. Hutchinson off here."

I shrugged. "They all stood me up. It happens."

"Mr. Murray's phone was found inside his car. Mr. Clarke and Mr. Hutchinson's phones were recovered a few miles from—"

"Lilli?" Mama called out through the intercom mounted on the parlor wall.

"Please excuse me for a moment. She probably needs to go to the restroom." I went over to the intercom and pressed the button. "Coming, Mama."

I returned to the parlor with a fresh pot of tea after I got Mama resettled. The detective stood at the mantle over the fireplace, looking at photos of Mama, Daddy, and me.

"Are you from here, Detective?" I set the tray down on the table. "I hope you don't mind the personal question."

"I'm from Atlanta. Took the job here about a year ago."

We both sat and I filled our cups. "I've heard Atlanta is a tough place to be a single Black woman looking to date Black men," I said. "But seriously, where isn't? If I may ask another personal question— because I don't want to be presumptuous, and I promise this is relevant to your investigation—do you date men?"

"Not since I moved here. And not for lack of trying. Why?"

"Then you know how hard it is. This town." I sighed. "Again, I know it's bad for us sisters everywhere, but here it's downright incestuous. My best friend and I joke that we're swapping the same five halfway decent guys back and forth between us. Not that any of that counts as *dating*. Dating requires effort, communication, common courtesy. That's the bare minimum, and if your 'dating' experiences have been anything like mine, you can't even get that. And then we're expected to just make a meal of crumbs without complaint. Be grateful for less than what we deserve. Weather all the chronic disregard unscathed and not need any tenderness."

I sipped my tea. The detective stared at her cup. "Those guys who are missing?" I said. "*They're* the perpetrators. The real victims here are *us*, Detective."

I looked at the time on my phone. "If you have any further questions for me, would you mind if we continued in the kitchen?" I asked. "I need to get dinner started so that Mama can be in bed by eight. I'm making linguine with white clam sauce and homemade garlic bread. Won't you stay for dinner?"

---

excerpt from Detective ▌▌▌▌▌'s Report

...All three missing persons were active on multiple online dating apps prior to their disappearances, and phone records indicate that between them, they stood up and/or "ghosted" and/or "breadcrumbed" dozens of local women, who were subsequently questioned as persons of interest. None of these women are currently considered persons of interest. In fact, in the course of their interviews, it was determined that the missing persons had, on countless occasions committed a crime, the crime of wasting a Black woman's time.

Sistas, how y'all feel?
Brothas, y'all alright?

CALLER

K-MING CHANG

WE MET OVER THE phone. She tried to scam me. She told me to contact the Nanjing Police Department because I was being investigated for financial crimes on the mainland. I don't have any finances, I told her, and also I'm Taiwanese. She laughed and switched to Hokkien: in that case, she told me, a package that is being delivered to you is now involved in a criminal investigation. Please call the Nanjing Police Department. She laughed again, and her voice over the phone sounded like it was being siphoned somewhere else at the same time. I loved this about her. I was always in her periphery, even when I was straddling her, my breast in her mouth, her tongue flicking my nipple as dismissively as if she were shutting off a light before leaving. If she were with me now, she would be looking at something behind me, the wall, the broken TV I never got fixed, the one my father used to watch medical shows on, even though I always told him not to watch them because they resulted in self-diagnosis, and once he called me three times in a night claiming to have kidney stones the size of his fists. You abstain from sodium, Baba, I told him. You're holding in your poop for too long again. Just go. Okay, he said, and later called me in the morning to say that I was correct, it was just that he was holding in his poop for too long. He had a fear of toilets, because one time as a child, when he was squatting in

a communal concrete outhouse, a hog charged in and nearly severed
his balls, and another time when he ran to the outhouse at night, he
saw a ghost squatting over the toilet, depositing the knotted scarf of
her intestines down the hole. After that, he had a fear of squatting for
anything, and refused to use any kind of public bathroom, including
one time when he took my sisters and me to Great America for our
shared birthday—he believed in communal birthdays—and ate four
blue raspberry snow cones and held it in until finally, when my sisters
and I exited the Top Gun–themed roller coaster for the sixth time in
a row, we found our father standing behind the public restroom, pee
seeping through the seam of his jeans, and we had to walk him back
to the parking lot, two of us standing in front of him and two of us
holding his hand, guiding him out like we were hired guards.

What kind of crime is my package being investigated for, I asked
the scammer on the phone. I didn't want her to hang up on me, and
my credit card number only provided access to my debt, so I figured
there was nothing she could subtract from me. The woman paused
and hummed, a sound that skimmed the back of my hands, then
said, Murder, I guess. Murder? I said. I am being sent something that
is involved in a murder? Yes, she replied, but she was laughing. Because I didn't know how to say it in Mandarin, I told her in English
that I thought she was supposed to be a robot. She laughed again,
and this time it sounded like it was coming from behind me, a laugh
that bejeweled my neck with sweat. No, she said in English, I'm not a
robot. But I know how to repeat myself. I told her there wasn't much
she could get out of me, that I worked at the post office sorting mail
into P.O. boxes and lived with six roommates, three of whom were
related to me, and she laughed again and said she knew. You don't
sound like what I need, she said, and now I wanted to convince her
that I was, that I was worth mining, that there was some kind of
pleasure I could produce for her. I told her my name was Tina, Na

pronounced the Chinese way. She told me we had similar names. My name is Liu Yina, she said. Yina, meaning "to perfect one million things." While I talked, I looked around the apartment I shared, the sink with its plaque I couldn't scrape off, the lightbulb in the center of the ceiling we never replaced even after it was shattered, the laid-out mattresses we mummified with plastic. My father always told me that cleanliness was the most important thing. That no matter where I lived, it should look like an oily forehead.

I asked Yina whether her scams ever worked. They're not *my* scams, she said. They're not my ideas. I have better ideas than this.

What kind of ideas, I asked her. The closest I'd ever come to a scam was when my father found out that the Whole Foods two towns over was giving out free Thanksgiving dinner sample platters the second week of November. He said we would go through the line first and snag our samples, and then we would wait for an employee shift and line up again. He even brought costumes along, a pair of dollar-store sunglasses for me, polka-dotted headbands for my sisters, a checkered fleece scarf he'd nicknamed British Man Being Casual. That was the first time my sisters and I ever had turkey, which we all decided was bland, salty in the way of snot, and should be significantly fattened. But it was the excitement of the disguise that returned us to the line all afternoon, the sunglasses that straddled my face and made me feel like I'd outgrown being seen, that I was an invisible deity among all the suckers who paid for dry meat.

I sat down on my mattress, careful not to reveal the sound of crackled plastic, and Yina said that her ideal scam would be a big one. She paused again. Her pauses weren't like other people's pauses, where you were still tuned into the static of their breath—her pauses were so clean and abrupt that it was like changing a channel, glitching between stories. Like that one on the mainland, she told me, about the man who impersonated a celebrity and talked online to this grandma and she believed him and gave him 1.9 million dollars. I said, why would a celebrity need money? And she said, that's the genius of it. He never even needed to ask. She gave over her money thinking it was a gift, thinking he'd never need it. That's the kind of scammer I want to be. The kind who doesn't need to ask, because they seem so above need that the very idea of their asking for anything feels impossible. That's the purest way, Yina said, none of this asking for credit card numbers, asking for bank account numbers, reaching your hand out and wriggling your fingers around. She loved him like a son and cared for him as one. He never had to beg her for anything because she was always convinced. You see? The best scams are like that. They're circumstantial. You don't do any work. My mother always said, don't try to wring out the sky. Go stand somewhere it's raining. Unzip your mouth.

I told her I'd never heard of that before. I wondered if I should be more disturbed by her admiration for a man who exploited the loneliness of an elderly woman who thought she was loved by someone who mattered, whose face fanned out on a screen, but I only wanted to keep unspooling her voice, to position myself somewhere in her sky. To be tricked. Convince me, I told her. Of what? she asked. Of anything, I said, I'm willing. She laughed and said I'd already punctured two of her scams, sullied her scripts. I want to meet you, I said. She said I sounded like law enforcement, and I told her that was the worst thing anyone had ever said to me. There are scammers in my family, too, I said. She made a sound in her throat that meant she didn't believe me, but I told her it was true. The longest scam, I said to her, longer than any scam you've ever pulled. I got married once.

Yina didn't ask me about it, though I wanted her to, I wanted her to be impressed by me, to comprehend the depth of my disguises, all the wants I'd worn and discarded. But instead she said she'd meet me. She gave me her address, and I was surprised that she'd be willing to meet a stranger in private, even though I'd been the first one to ask. I'm not worried about you, she said. You're a scammer too.

She lived in an apartment alone, twice the size of the one I shared with my roommates, and the building was located beside a highway. It was a two-hour drive to get there, and I'd passed two landfills and a waste processing center and a swamp that smelled like beef. When Yina answered the door—she lived on the ground floor, which impressed me—I almost told her that my father used to work at that waste processing center, that he used to pluck anything that wouldn't decompose off a conveyor belt, which was mostly everything. He wore a plastic visor and gloves and a blue full-body suit with silver knees that made him resemble a cartoon astronaut, and he joked that that was where he worked, on an alien planet where no one traversed. In elementary school, a teacher showed our class a picture of the surface of Mars, and I almost called out that I'd seen the surface of that world, that it looked related to the landfill at the city's brim, an estranged sibling.

But I said nothing, and Yina answered the door in her pajamas, pink plaid with moth-colored lace hemming the cuffs of her pants. Her apartment was colonized by light, lamps in every corner, her single window open, no curtains. There was a futon in the center of the room, rolled out flat, large enough for an entire family. I sleep wide, Yina said, I sleep like a murdered person, you know, all my limbs in different places. She laughed, and I realized that her voice was different in person, that she rattled the words in her mouth like dice before spitting them out, gambling away their meaning, careless with every beginning. She manifested a can of Hong Van and handed it to me. It was room temperature and the can was dented in at the H. I asked if she remembered the old Hong Van commercials on KTSF, where the woman in the white bikini swings over the sea. It was the only time I ever paid attention to what was on TV: when the woman

stretched out her teeth-white legs and sang about something so sweet
it could sanctify your mouth. Yes, I remember, she said. I used to run
a scam on there. What kind of scam, I asked her. A church one, she
said, not explaining anymore.

I sipped from the can of Hong Van and sat on the edge of her
futon. She said I had very small hands, and I looked down at them.
Not really, I said, I just like holding things with two hands. Safer. She
laughed and said I was the same in person. You're so honest, she said,
you could have just hung up. But instead you said you had nothing
to give me.

I really don't, I replied, but it was a lie. Already I was moving
toward her, reaching down for the back of her knee so that it would
bend for me. When I brushed my thumbs against her earlobes, her
lips unknit. It's so easy, she said with her head tilted back, to get
people to say yes to me. You just have to sound needy. People respond
to need. They can't help it. It's worse than gravity. On the futon,
I crouched between her legs, steering my tongue up the length of
her thigh, licking the seam of her plaid pajama pants. I wondered
if somehow this was part of a long scam I didn't know about, that
this is where she'd been trying to navigate me from the beginning.
Her neck was pale as pith and I wanted to teethe into it. I believed
that she had once been on TV. Outside, the rain was repeating us,
saying my words to the pavement: please, please. I shed my shirt
and it coiled on her futon like a snake. My father loved to tell stories
about disguises, like that one about the woman who scammed a man
into marrying her, then accidentally revealed she was a white snake. I
think the ending of the story was that he killed her for her deception,
but maybe that was just the one my father chose, the warning he
wrapped around the real ending, waiting for me to undress it.

Yina fucked me with her fingers. I was on all fours, my head
dangling down, sliding myself onto her. She leaned over me, nipping

the back of my neck, petting my shoulders with her other hand, telling me to breathe. There was something diagnostic about the way she touched me, as if she was measuring the depth of me. I expected her to stop and say aha, this is it, I found this inside you, here it is, but I couldn't imagine the shape of the thing. Later, lying side by side, her hands ornamented with wet, I asked her how she became a scammer, if it was something she enjoyed. She laughed and said that was a very American thing to ask. Whether labor was enjoyable. There's no such thing, she said. Making money is making money. Right, I said, but you could do something else. You have a choice to do something else.

Something more ethical, I wanted to say. She paused, then asked me what I did. I wondered if she was asking me again to confirm my identity, if this was some sort of security question. I work part-time at the postal office, I said, sorting mail. Yina laughed and said I was an enabler, then, since most of the scams she used to work for were mail-based. Do you ever think about opening someone else's mail? It was easier, talking to her without looking at her, her hips grazing mine, her lamps laying out our shadows to dry and curl away. No, I said, it's just a job. Though, I said to her, one time I was sorting this envelope. It was bumpy, unpadded. I didn't think it was that unusual, I thought maybe it was jewelry, but there was something about the shape inside it that bothered me. I held the envelope up to the light—it was always too bright inside the post office, like we were perpetually getting scanned for something, and I realized, as I was feeling the ridges of the envelope, that it was full of teeth. Teeth? Yina asked. Yes, I said, it was full of teeth. Just teeth. No sheets of paper, no letter, anything like that. It was just an envelope full of teeth.

Yina turned onto her side and looked at me, her teeth tugging my ear. She spoke so close that her words were breath-blurred, inseparable. Sometimes pulling a scam is like that, she said, like pulling teeth. The first scam I ever pulled, I was thirteen. I was in love with this girl whose family made geese.

Do you mean they bred geese? No, Yina said, they made geese. It was fake goosemeat, something synthetic, but they sold it as real and we all ate it. My mother says that's why my breasts are so small, because I ate fake meat. Anyway, Yina said, I was in love with her because she had long hair all the way down to her knees and she had straight teeth and she was my neighbor. She could also make geese sounds and it made me laugh, even though I hate geese because they bite your ass. But anyway, whenever we went out together she pretended to be a boy. It worked until high school, almost. She had the most beautiful voice I ever heard. It was lower than an earthquake. She could swear like a boy and smoke like one. She'd ask big men for cigarettes and they gave them to her. Because she asked in that voice, the one with the motor, the one that moved light.

Yina laughed. But a scam can't last forever, she said. It was the last thing Yina said to me before we fell asleep and I went home and I forgot to look closely again at the garbage plant that pulsed between our parts of the city, the place where my father had donated one of his thumbs to the mechanized sorting machine. It shouldn't matter what goes where, Baba had said to me, it all gets buried. Clamped between my knees was a can of Hong Van, frothing and fermented, the jewels of grass jelly thrumming inside.

The next morning, I left for my shift at the post office. Twice that week, my father had called me saying that he'd been watching a YouTube video about cysts. What kind of cysts, I asked him, and he said he didn't really know, he had his eyes closed most of the time, but anywhere inside of you the cysts can nest, like those idiot birds that keep clustering in his walls and that he had to core out every spring. Okay, I said, cysts are dangerous, eat less sodium, and tell me if something bursts. I told him I'd come home soon, but it was harder in person, harder to pretend I believed him. That was something Yina

said, that it was easier to scam someone over the phone, to dangle
something at a distance, because your face is what makes the mistake.
Your face gives it away, she says. Everything you want is welded to it.
I'd turned away from her on the futon and asked her what mistake
my face was making right that moment. It's turned away from me,
she said, and I laughed, turning back around so that she could tuck
her thumb beneath my tongue.

Each time I picked up the phone, I thought it might be Yina
dressed in my father's voice, executing some part of her master scam.
But she didn't call again, and I drove to the post office every morning
in my blue uniform, the same shade as my father's old one. When he
first heard that my job was sorting something, he warned me against
the sawteeth of machines. It's sorting mail, not trash, I said, trying to
reassure him. It's sorting things that are wanted. I didn't realize that
that might hurt him, but he never asked about my job again. The post
office parking lot was half empty, and when I walked into the fluorescent back room, the wheeled bins were full to the brim. I stood in front
of the PO boxes like a row of cavities and began to fill them, flicking
through the mail tub, my eyes skimming the numbers, the names. My
thumb snagged on one of the envelopes, smaller than the standard size,
the body of it bulging. It was addressed to me, just my name and the
address of the post office below it, no box number, no return address.
The handwriting was small and knotted, each letter knocking against
the next. I knew it was hers: she wrote the same way she spoke, waiting
for me to do the work of unraveling, to tug at each word until it tore.
I held the envelope with both hands. It was pebbled, the paper rippled
and rained-on. I lifted it to the light, but I already knew what was
inside. I recognized her molar mounting my nipple, the graze of her
canines against my knuckles. Through the paper, I pressed my thumb
against the cliff of a tooth, soliciting blood and sweeping its shadow
across the envelope, disguising my name with a stain.

ALL YOU HAVE IS YOUR FIRE

YAH YAH SCHOLFIELD

IT STARTED WITH THE toolshed. It wasn't an impressive structure, her father having built it using only scrap wood and metal. The nails were bent, and the wood was warped from the rain, discolored. The toolshed was small, twenty by twenty feet at most, bereft of tools but filled to the brim with furniture and moving boxes. The ground was soft and damp beneath Dahlia's bare feet, and the dank smell of sodden cardboard and wet earth irritated her nose. Every so often, a cool breeze cut through the slats of the wood, making a high, whistling noise that both soothed and frightened her.

At fourteen, Dahlia was pimpled and pockmarked, mortified by her body and even more so by her mind. She had thoughts that sometimes took her body by force. Once, she broke a plate just to hear it shatter. Another time, she ran out into the road, laid down on the asphalt, and waited for something to happen.

That night wasn't her fault, though. Supposedly, she had said something "smart" to her mother. There was a flurry of motion, a slap across her mouth, and the jangle of a belt buckle as the leather zipped through the belt loops. Whippings usually subdued Dahlia, but this time she was angry, caught off guard by the violence and stunned by the insult of leather against her skin. What had she done so wrong? Speak too frankly? Breathe too loud?

Her father, interpreting Dahlia's quiet anger as defiance, took her by the arm, dragged her out of the house, and marched her out to the toolshed. The door was pulled open—stale air pushed *out*—and Dahlia was thrown inside. She fell to her hands and knees, the flesh of her palms scraped raw against the wood chips. Her body stung, ripped and stripped, everything open to the elements. Even so, Dahlia kept her head down low, chest burning something awful. She wanted to cry, but she refused to do so in front of her father. To be punished was to be humiliated. To admit defeat with tears and whimpers was pure cowardice, proof that she could be broken.

Dahlia stayed on her knees until her father left the shed. She heard the lock click from the outside.

"You'll get let out when you learn how to respect your elders," said her father.

Only when she was alone did she allow herself to scream. She could make noise, dear Dahlia. She yelled, banged on the wood door, kicked her feet and shrieked. She didn't ache. Ache was something for the belly, for the head, and those could be soothed. No, Dahlia *hurt*. She felt weak and simple, wrung dry and left flapping in the musty air of the toolshed. Her heart beat violently at its confines, thumping, pressing. She wheezed as she slammed against the door.

"Let me out! Let me out! Let *me out!*"

Oh, but who was listening? Who would come for her? Dahlia knew better than anybody that her carrying on was in vain. Her daddy didn't care what happened to her; disciplining the children, raising the children, was for the woman to do. Her mama? As if she would admit she was wrong, Bible-backed and stubborn, to any kind of fault. And her siblings were no help either. They were too young, and the ones that weren't still clinging to Mama for comfort were meek, pressed low, too afraid of the belt to risk breaking her out. No one would come for her. If she was smart (and she was extremely smart), she'd conserve her strength and bide her time. Suck in the sawdust and puff out plumes of dust until somebody saw fit to release her. Dahlia quieted, panting. She checked her hands for splinters and pulled gravel from her palms. She rounded the small space of the shed, peeking into boxes and nosing through plastic bins. Dahlia didn't feel sorry for herself; she didn't like to feel pitiful. She pulled down some bent boxes and dug through them. In this one was VHS of first steps, first birthdays, and family events. In that one, faded photographs of her mother and father, unsmiling, standing near each other without touching on their wedding day. And over there, in the one with the stickers slapped onto its side, were old toys of hers, church programs gone limp with age, cassettes with loose streams of tape and polaroids from decades ago. Curiously, carefully, Dahlia unwound a fine gauzy thing she discovered to be a veil. She marveled at it, coughed from the dust as she settled it over her head, mindful of her braids.

Adorned like a bride and draped in the dust of memories, Dahlia mined through the boxes until she found the box of matches. Darkness was folding in, slipping through the gaps of the shed's fragile structure. Dahlia squinted to see the fine details of the box. On its front, cats gathered around the table with their brown humanoid paws extended to each other so that they touched. She was cautious with the box, nervous of the striking edge, but curious too. She brought the box close to her face, observed it. The cats were all tabbies, sly-faced and smiling cheekily at one another, a clever secret balanced on each of their thin whiskers. The cat at the center of the group looked directly at Dahlia, teasing her with its yellow eyes.

Outside the shed, the world was turning into itself for sleep. Yellow-orange sunset filtered through the wood slats, then night, then the incessant chatter of the cicadas and crickets. Insect song rang out all around her, near enough to unsettle but somehow far enough to be a soothing sound. Outside her mother was turning off the house lights one by one, dousing the life from each of the rooms.

Dahlia selected a match. It was unremarkable—a plain stick of wood with a bright red wig of sulfur. She remembered, from her father showing her, how to light a match. He preferred the drama of the flicking wrist, the scratch of red against red, to the lighters her mother favored. Dahlia, forbidden to tamper with fire unsupervised, had formed no opinion as of yet. She only knew that the match was boring and small, and that her hand shook a little as she struck it.

It took a few tries to catch. Dahlia struck three times before it burned steadily, and when it did, the flame was fine and lovely. A germ of power was planted into her. Dahlia stared hungrily at the light. It was nothing but hot air, orange and yellow, inoffensive yet dangerous. Delicious. She held it close to her face and watched as it burned down to the tips of her fingers. The fire singed her. Dahlia cried out, dropped what remained of the stick and sucked on the hurt fingers. She stomped on the match, petulant, annoyed, but she removed herself from the pain and returned to her box of tabbies.

Dahlia lit six matches in all. They burned in her fingers, some burning flesh and some nothing but air. The smoke stung her eyes, but she lit them still. At the sixth match, Dahlia's germ of power burst into a green sprout. She brought the flame over to a box of photographs and dropped it in, watching as the flames devoured the pictures, the box that held them, the ground covered in sawdust and wood chips.

According to her parents, it was an accident. She didn't *mean* to burn down the toolshed. She was desperate and cold, dimwitted in the darkness. Of course, it was not mentioned why Dahlia was in the shed so late at night, and if it was, the story was changed to a troubled girl sneaking out the house, too wily to be stopped. And though Dahlia knew the stories weren't true, she accepted them. Most fairy tales were changed to become sweeter, softer, more palatable. Let her story change too, from mermaid dissolving into sea foam to a happily ever after. She changed her memory to exclude the beauty of the box of tabbies, the beauty of the fire, the warmth, the excitement, how thrilling it was to let the matches burn low in her fingers, and how, even though the flames grew hotter and higher, she stood with her back to the door of the shed, knowing that she would be burned soon but doing nothing to stop it.

∽℘∼

She read *Firestarter* when she was fifteen, then *Carrie* when she was a year older. Dahlia stole a copy of *We Have Always Lived in The Castle* from the big library downtown, and snatched *The Haunting of Hill House*, *Beloved*, *Flowers in the Attic*, and a few others a week later. These were secular books, dark and unholy, their yellowed pages filled with nudity and sex and violence. Forbidden, foreboding; Dahlia kept them in a locked trunk beneath her bed, shoved too deep for her mother to reach them. She brought them out only when she was home alone.

She was drawn to these books—girls with powers, girls who were monstrous, girls who had the potential to be terrible and violent things. She thrilled at the description of Beloved's creaking voice, *soared* over each and every act of cruelty from Corrine Foxworth. Carrie sent knives through the body of her mother, piercing her like St. Sebastian, and Dahlia had to steel herself against the force of her imaginings. How delicious these women were! How deadly and heartless! Oh, when Sethe took a blade to the neck of her dear baby—Dahlia threw the book across the room, hands shaking, eyes closed. She could imagine, she could imagine.

Dahlia knew she was nothing like Carrie, like Charlene, like Sethe, like Corrine, like Merricat or Beloved or Eleanor. She was not damned with any sort of abilities. Her mind was not beset by ghosts.

She had no ancient home, lived in no attic and kept no mysterious manor. The toolshed (gone now) was once her prayer closet, and there were candles, and sometimes she felt a deadly urge to scream and cuss, but she couldn't dart her eyes and crumble buildings.

Her violence was old fashioned. She lit matches and she burned things. She built a collection of lighters, a collection of accelerants that she kept in plastic bottles hidden around her room. All buildings were good buildings to be burned, but Dahlia most liked the ones that were falling apart anyway. It was like she was God, striking out, sending bolts of lightning to destroy.

After the toolshed, Dahlia experimented with other sheds of the same size. The neighbors' first, and then a dilapidated greenhouse in the community garden. The first building-building she burned was an abandoned house a few blocks away from her own home. She passed it every day coming home from school, and fell in love with its busted-out windows and rotting walls. Dahlia didn't think there were any people living in it, though sometimes during her exploratory walks in the house she saw beer bottles and blankets.

But remainders of human life did not mean anyone was there. Dahlia recalled being spooked off from a particularly exciting broken-down Victorian after seeing a handful of cigarette butts on the porch. Only later did she understand her caution was useless; teenage boys came to smoke there and often left their trash behind. There was nothing to fear in a forgotten house.

Mind made up, Dahlia began her process. First, she collected gasoline, siphoning a little at a time from her father's car and scoring the rest from a distracted gas station attendant. The matches were purchased from a convenience store, chosen for the picture of a woman smoking on the box's cover. The sensuality and dichotomy of it intrigued her—two pretty ladies burning things down, one with a cigarette in her mouth and the other with braces.

She came to the house at night. It wasn't difficult escaping her room. Her father rarely asked after her, having long ago sworn her off, and her mother had all but erased Dahlia. When she slipped down from her bedroom window and out into the night, she was invisible, unknowable, accompanied only by her own shadow.

Quickly and quietly, concealed by darkness, she moved through the rooms, dousing the broken furniture in gasoline. Dahlia saw where she would start—in the upstairs bedroom, the gauzy and moth-eaten curtains sure to go up in moments. The rooms spread out in front of her as she imagined the path the fire would take, what fabric it would devour. *What fabric* I'll *devour*, and she let the thought warm her through, until she was a bulb of light flashing from place to place, gently tapping things and turning them red.

While she walked, she saw other things, more bottles and blankets, a case of near-rotten fruits tucked into a cabinet. Dahlia pushed these aside with her shoe and went on, splashing gas around her feet.

Now came the delicious part. Dahlia removed the pack of matches—plain, skinny blonde sticks with redheads, nothing at all like the tantalizing pack of matches from the toolshed—and struck it hard against the side. The flame danced up and up, waggling its red-and-orange head. Dahlia brought the first flame to the curtains. Like she thought, it caught quickly, flying up the length of the fabric in lines of blue and orange, ashes shaking down as the flame ate away at it. She moved slowly then, striking and bringing matches to each place she tapped before. By the time she made it to the smallest of the upstairs bedrooms, Dahlia's face was wet with sweat, and she was trembling from the smoke and heat. Still, she pushed on, lighting and ruining.

She came down the stairs and lit them after her, then the living room, then a little sunroom covered in kudzu. Upstairs, a window burst, or a mirror. She thrilled at the crashing, smashing noises of the fire going from destructive to dangerous. See how fearsome she was, how powerful and wicked.

Dahlia took her gas can, the empty box of matches, and went outside. She stood close to the street, handmade flames illuminating her face and glaring brightly in her eyes. The urge to light a match and burn her own hand, just so she could match the perfect glow, was almost too consuming to resist. She dug her fingers into her arm instead, bouncing a little on her heels as the house came down.

It was devasting, it was beautiful. Then she saw the pillar of fire run screaming out of the house.

THE OTHER YOU

MAISY CARD

YOU HAVE PATROLLED THE street where the Old Wife lives for five days. You've tried to stagger the times between loops around the block, but since you know from your husband that the Old Wife is the kind of woman who watches her neighbors incessantly through her front windows, you assume that she's noticed you by now, wondered about that strange woman who keeps passing her house.

❧

You sat in your rental car for the first few days, waiting for the Old Wife to open her door. Every day around noon, you've watched as the Old Wife walks across her veranda, hesitating before unlocking the iron grillwork gate, and then step out onto the grass barefoot. Wearing a dress that was in fashion thirty years before, she waits. The Old Wife's dresses have been washed so often that the patterns are almost nonexistent. Today, you stare at the white dress with the barely visible yellow flowers, and from your rental car, you watch the Old Wife looking out at the road. You can feel the internal prayer the woman recites, hoping he will come.

❧

The Old Wife's skin is pale and her eyes are light. From a far-ther distance, you might have mistaken her for a white woman. You smiled when you saw that her hair had already gone gray, and that the Old Wife is so careless that she hasn't bothered to dye it. Your hair has remained black, even after twenty years of marriage, except for a few strays that you pluck each week. The Old Wife's face is gaunt. She appears to be nothing but skin and bones beneath her dress. As you watch her frail, small figure waiting on the grass, you're grate-ful that your flesh has expanded with age, that until recently, you have longed for nothing. Even from across the road, you can discern her shallow sigh, feel that moment of disappointment when the Old Wife realizes that the man she's been waiting for, your husband, isn't there.

∽◉∽

You haven't set foot in Jamaica for more than twenty years. You should be enjoying the sun, visiting family. You told your husband that your Uncle Raymond died—a truth—but also that you would be attending the funeral—a lie.

∽◉∽

You were married to your husband for twenty years before you found a picture of the Old Wife, the one he abandoned in Jamaica when he married you. Your husband lied to you, told you that he burned them all. He told you that the Old Wife was dead to him, which seemed fitting, forgivable, since the Old Wife believes that her husband is dead, that he died years ago. She's unaware that he's been living with you, under a different name, in New York. When you looked at the picture of the Old Wife for the first time, posing next to a younger version of your husband in her wedding dress, and the one he kept of his infant daughter, staring at you with big saintly hazel eyes, wearing nothing but her brown skin and her nappy, another picture formed in your mind. You could see your husband rotting in his grave. You knew it was the one that the Old Wife carried in her mind too.

∽≀∽

You have the urge to get closer, and today you finally get the courage. You have a hotel room, but last night you decided to sleep in your rental car, just to see if the Old Wife receives any visitors during the night. She doesn't. As you slam the car door and walk toward the house, you plan what you will say.

The stray dogs have gotten so comfortable with you that they no longer bark when you walk up and down the street, or when you stop for a few minutes to stare directly at the Old Wife's house. They no longer keep their distance. On the first day, they were only brave enough to deliver a warning to you from across the road. The dogs trail behind you now, whimpering, begging for food. At first, when you saw the way they fell asleep each day on the sidewalk directly in front of the Old Wife's house, you wondered if she was the one who fed them, who caused them to take up permanent residence on this street.

∽≀∽

For a brief moment, you had formed an impression of the Old Wife, one contrary to the one given to you by your husband, one of her being nurturing and kind. But toward the evening, your second day patrolling the Old Wife's street, the old man directly across from

her house came outside in nothing but a T-shirt and a pair of saggy
briefs and tossed the animals some dried-up pieces of cornmeal por-
ridge. "Is who you out here every day lookin' fah?" he finally asked.
"Nobody," you answered, and walked to your car, pretending to drive
away, only to circle the block until he'd gone back inside.

∽◦∽

You have watched the neighbors gather in each other's yards to
gossip after coming home from work each evening. They bring each
other pieces of rum cake or plates of stew chicken and rice and peas
so that their friends have some respite from their own kitchens. But
no one steps into the Old Wife's yard, no one ever knocks on her
door. A young girl goes to market in the early morning, then remains
inside for the rest of the day. A man occasionally cuts the grass. Except for the half an hour a day that she spends outside, waiting for
your husband, she doesn't stand on her veranda or by her front gate
with any expectation of a greeting like her neighbors do. You didn't
expect the Old Wife to be such a recluse. You know that if you don't
meet her today, you'll have to let another full day go by before you
see her again. You've told your husband that you'll be gone for only
seven days.

∽◦∽

When you see her today, the Old Wife is still wearing the same
dress as the day before. Her gray hair hasn't been combed. The young
helper follows her out of the house, and you can tell that she's trying
to urge her back inside, but the Old Wife swats at her furiously, as if
she's a swarm of flies. The girl backs away and scurries into the house.
When you cross the street and come to stand with one hand on the

Old Wife's gate, the woman just turns and walks over to a bush of orange hibiscus growing in the corner of her front yard.

∾◉⌒

You want to tell her the truth. Several truths, in fact, even though it's clear that the Old Wife has no wish to hear them. First, that Stanford, the friend of her dead husband who has been writing her letters for the past few months, is not coming to see her as he promised. Second, that he cannot because it was actually you who wrote those letters, pretending to be him. And finally, that the Old Wife's dead husband and your living husband are one and the same. You want to tell her, but you wonder if the Old Wife has already lost her mind. She refuses to look at you, even when you wave. Instead, the Old Wife plucks a flower and closes her eyes as she brings it to her nose, with a desperate focus, as though she can sense you there but regards you as a mere apparition that she can ward away.

∾◉⌒

This is the first time you feel guilt. Why have you been fantasizing about the Old Wife grasping at the hem of your dress, pleading with you to admit that what you've told her isn't true? Why have you been imagining the Old Wife collapsing with grief? Why do you want to watch the woman tear her hair out in disbelief? Is it because you want to feel the Old Wife's desire for your husband, because maybe then you could feel it again too? As it stands, all your desire for that man has left you, but you don't know how to follow. You don't know how to leave him.

∾◉⌒

You wanted to grasp at the hem of the woman, the girl, still in her twenties, who came to your store months ago to tell you that she is pregnant by your husband. The possibility never entered your mind that dead men could get women pregnant. You thought it was only you. You thought he gave you a daughter because you were the only person alive who knew his secret, who could see him for who he really was.

⌖

You had wanted to slap the girl's face, attack her eyes with your acrylic nails, but instead you just stood there, behind the register, with your mouth open, while she made a fool of you. *He's gonna pay for this child*, she said, loud enough for your customers to hear. And when you stuttered a bit before telling her to get out of your store, the girl laughed in your face. She was as young as you had been when you married your husband. After all those years, you'd never imagined that it would be so easy for him to find another you. It never occurred to you before then that perhaps you were just another version of the Old Wife. You were a poor man's version of her back then, but at least you were young. After the young girl who was carrying your husband's child left the store, you went home and found the Old Wife's picture in the hiding place in the attic, and you wrote her a letter.

⌖

As you wait for the Old Wife to lower the flower and open her eyes, you stare at the paint on the front of her house, which is as faded as her dress. When you first arrived, you could tell from the stench that wafts from her yard that she keeps livestock in the back.

You wondered how the Old Wife survived without your husband. You imagined that she took in sewing like your mother and grandmother did before, in desperation, they sent you, a single teenage girl, to London to work. On your second day in Jamaica, you'd seen one of the Old Wife's neighbors leave for work and you'd climbed over his fence and walked around to the back to confirm. There, you could look into the Old Wife's yard. It was bigger than expected. Big enough for a wide chicken coop and a pen full of goats, with room for a grove of fruit trees. The man who cut the grass was feeding the animals, so you ducked behind a tree. You didn't realize that your husband abandoned such a solid house on a decent piece of land. You found yourself jealous of a woman who sells milk and eggs and animal flesh to survive.

How can you be jealous of the Old Wife when she has nothing and you have everything? Yes, the Old Wife had a white wedding dress made of lace and a veil that covered her face. You only had two good dresses when you met the Old Wife's husband in London, both made of cheap polyester, and the two of you couldn't even scrape together the money to put a fresh relaxer in your hair before the ceremony.

But now, you have U.S. citizenship. In a few short years, you'll have a pension from working as a nurse for the VA. You own a home in Harlem and a grocery store. The Old Wife's letters back to your husband were desperate and sad: *Dear Stanford, it is good to hear from someone who knew Abel. Each time I read your letter it brings me back to life. I haven't been in good health and my children don't care for me properly.*

∽๏๛

You had once thought that him letting the Old Wife believe he was dead, and that you going along with it, was cruel. Now you understand how much crueler it is to have a liar still crawling in your bed at night. To have a liar sleep soundly next to you. You want someone to share this burden of having a liar for a husband.

You clear your throat loudly, standing at the Old Wife's gate. It is obvious that you want to talk to her, yet she won't look away from the hibiscus, as if she knows already that your intentions are not good.

"Vera?" You say, the first time you've said the Old Wife's name, so alien in your mouth, like speaking an unknown language aloud for the first time. She looks up then, spends too long staring at you as if you might be someone she knows.

"Yes? I'm Vera," she says finally. Her accent isn't thick compared to those of her neighbors. Your husband told you that the Old Wife came from a family with money, and you can hear the remnants of that life in her voice.

"Stanford nah come no more, but him send me instead."

You can see her thinking, turning over this new knowledge in her mind then conceiving a polite way to get rid of you.

"Him give me some things to give you." You tap your handbag and pull it toward you, clutching it firmly as if you're holding something precious inside.

Your husband has taught you how to lie. He does not know how much you have learned from him. He believed you when you told him that you were going to Jamaica for your uncle's funeral. He cannot go back to Jamaica because he is dead. Dead men don't walk the streets of their youth in broad daylight. Dead men cannot visit your family. So he makes you call him every day to report what you did, who you've seen. More chances to practice your lying. By the time you meet the Old Wife face to face, it comes easily.

The Old Wife doesn't tell you to follow her. At first, you fear that she sees right through you, that she's not convinced. She merely turns and walks back to her veranda, where she sits in a wicker chair and stares at you through the bars. You eventually walk across the yard to sit in the chair across from her. The Old Wife does not offer drink or food, doesn't call to the young helper to cater to you. Now that you are close, you can see how far away she is from the woman in the picture. You wonder if your husband would even recognize her, if she would recognize him if they passed each other on the street.

"Why he never come himself?" she asks, forcing you to think of an excuse on the spot. The Old Wife's voice is surprisingly high-pitched. You try to imagine her shrieking after you tell her.

"There was no one to mind the store," you say.

"Why didn't you mind it for him?" You don't need to explain that you are his wife. She's seen the wedding ring on your finger, and she already knows. You know that you've been backed into a corner, so you don't try to justify your coming. Instead you reach into your purse and hand her the letter, a final letter that you have written to the Old Wife under your own name. You have placed it in a special envelope that you bought from a stationery store. The Old Wife takes it, turns it over, admiring the special paper, the gold-leaf edges, and smiles. She opens the flap carefully, planning to save it.

Dear Vera,

I want you to know that I am writing this letter because I'm a god-fearing woman who believes in loyalty, faith, and truth above all else. I would like to ask your forgiveness for taking part in my husband's betrayal of you. My husband's name as you've heard is Stanford, but contrary to what the other letters you've received have said, and what you've been led to believe, he was not a friend of your husband Abel. He is Abel. He has been living under this name all of these years, a fact that I've been fully aware of and have done nothing to stop. I'm here to ask for your forgiveness. I hope I'm not too late to repair the wrong that has been done to you. Your husband Abel is alive, living in New York, and with the exception of a few minor health issues, he is well. If you would like to get in touch with him, I will do my best to make that reunion possible.

Sincerely,
Adele Solomon

You watch as she reads the letter, or at least you think that she is reading the letter, until she turns it over and looks at the blank side. She flips it over again, seems to be rereading it, then hands it back to you.

"Them did tell me say Abel get crush by one shipping container," she says, standing and looking over your head as if there's someone behind you. You turn and look through the bars that enclose the veranda, at the yard beyond to make sure. You see a flash of anger contort the Old Wife's features, directed at that space above you, but the tears that you are waiting for do not come. Instead, the Old Wife opens her front door and goes into the house without inviting you to follow, but you do.

The house is so dark inside, you have to pause and wait for your eyes to adjust. You're surprised to find it so clean, though the furniture, like the clothes, is the standard from decades ago. You don't see her and you realize that she's probably gone into her bedroom, the only room with the door closed. You stand in front of the kitchen where the helper is hovering over the stove, waiting for her to notice you. The girl looks up at you and startles, but then she smiles, and you wonder if she's excited to finally have a visitor.

"Miss Vera need fi sleep. She never take her insulin today," she says. "Me just give it to her."

You don't know what to do. You're not sure if it's an invitation to stay and wait or a hint to leave, so you just sit down at the table. The girl is making curry chicken, your husband's favorite meal. You close your eyes and imagine your husband in this house. Before he was your husband, before he was a liar, when he was still secure in his other life. When you open them, Vera is standing above you.

"I did think I dream you," she says, smiling.

"You ready to eat?" the helper asks her. The Old Wife looks into the pot and scowls, then she looks at you.

"Come, let we go outside." You stand up to follow. "Wait," she says. "Let me get my purse." You move to the hallway, expecting the two of you to go out the front door, but instead you hear her calling you from the kitchen. The back door is open. She steps out into the yard and you follow her. The helper says something to you as you pass her but you can't make it out.

"Adele is a pretty name," the Old Wife says to you in the yard. Now she's cradling a brown leather purse as if it's a child. You don't know what else to do except nod.

"I like the name Vera," you say in a quiet voice. "That was my grandmother's name."

"Oh really!" The Old Wife, Vera, releases one hand from her purse and squeezes your arm, gleefully.

You smile and then suddenly change your composure. This is not what you expected to happen.

"This dream is different," the Old Wife says, nodding, as if reading your mind.

"What dream?"

"You nuh know how many time I have this dream?"

"What dream?" you ask her again.

"Ever since Abel die, I dream that somebody'll come to me and tell me that him not really dead."

"This is not one dream." You grab her by both of her shoulders. You're disturbed by the distant look in her eyes. "This is real. I come here to tell you that your husband is not dead." Vera looks at you and smiles in a patronizing way, as if you are a simple child, naïve, innocent. You want to tell her that you were those things when you married her husband. That he took them away from you.

"When I get the letter from Stanford, I think I know what going to happen. I think that he the one who supposed to tell me, but this dream is different," she says. "This the first time one woman come to tell me."

Vera opens her purse. She pulls out a stack of envelopes.

"The angel always tell me the same thing."

"Angel? Vera, you nuh hear yourself? Me not one angel."

"Him never look like angel. Him always look like ordinary man. But him always tell me the same thing. Him say Abel nuh dead, but God see fit to save him from me. You know Jeremiah?"

"Me nuh know nobody name Jeremiah."

"Jeremiah chapter 4, verse 30: *What are you doing, you devastated one? Why dress yourself in scarlet and put on jewels of gold? Why highlight your eyes with makeup? You adorn yourself in vain. Your lovers despise you; they want to kill you.*"

Vera throws the letters on the ground. Then she reaches into her purse and pulls out another fistful.

"Me nuh understand," you tell her.

"The whole time Abel did in England, I write him letter to send me money, send me clothes. Send me everything. No wonder God take him 'way from me. No wonder him nuh wan' to come back."

She throws the purse itself on the pile. There's a shed made out of corrugated metal in the far corner of the yard, next to the goat pen.

You watch Vera go into the shed and come back with a glass bottle containing some light yellow liquid.

"Wait," you say, before she can pour the liquid. "Vera, me say is not dream you dreaming. This is real."

"I did know one day it would be real. You never have premonition before? God never send you them kind of dream?"

"No," you say, and for some reason you feel ashamed.

Vera motions with her head for you to move aside. You watch Vera pour the liquid all over the letters. She pulls a small box of matches out of her dress pocket and lights it. The fire catches fast, rises quickly. You both watch in silence as the paper burns.

"Wait," you say. You take off your wedding ring and throw it in the fire.

Vera starts laughing.

"Is what you laughing after?" you ask.

"Fire not gonna burn gold. You that fool? You nuh know that?"

You look away from her, humiliated. When you turn back, Vera is standing closer to the fire. She takes a step forward and a flame catches onto her dress and races up the fabric. You throw yourself onto her without thinking, roll on the ground. You scream for help.

∽◎⌒

Vera makes no sound as the girl puts ointment on her burns, as she cleans the mud off her. You help her into a clean nightgown and the two of you put her to bed.

You sit at the kitchen table with your head down, overcome by exhaustion. When you lift your head, your ring and the letter that you came to give Vera are in front of you.   The ring seems to sparkle more than ever, like the fire gave it the polish that it had been longing for. The girl is walking toward you with a plate of food.

"Is why you cryin'?" she asks with indignation, as she sets it in front of you, in between you and your ring, like you have done something to insult her. You are holding the letter to Vera and you decide to hand it to the girl, to give it to Vera again when she wakes. You offer it to her, but she turns her back to you. She brings you a knife and fork, places them before you, still eyeing the letter with suspicion.

"Take it," you say, but the girl just looks at you without moving. "Take it!" you command, wishing you could force all your earthly burdens on this child.

MAPS

VANESSA CHAN

WHEN YOU DIE, I become obsessed with recreating you. I walk endlessly through our town, to notable places in your life. I go to our old school where you were bullied relentlessly by girls who were skinnier and smaller than you because unlike me, you refused to be quiet and accept their ridicule. I go to the stationery store where you would buy those glitter pens that leaked on everything and gave you purple patches on the pocket of your school uniform shirt, to the mailbox where you used to mail the letters you wrote to your pen-pal in the prison program, to the gas station bathroom where you told me you once shit without touching your butt to the seat but then your shit bounced so hard into the bowl it splattered dirty gas station toilet water all over your ass. I stroll to the playground where you blew a boy in front of me as he sat on the swing and you knelt on the sand under him; to your old house where you said you touched a penis for the first time when your father made you touch his.

You are my sister, you said once when I was six and you were five and a half and I rolled my eyes, ever the skeptic, always trying to assert myself as the smarter one. No, silly, we're not related by *blood*, I said. Your face fell and I watched your cheeks crumple in that familiar way that I knew portended a loud storm of tears, so I quickly retreated. Fine, fine, we can be sisters, I said, and you were happy, and the sun crept back into your eyes.

Every day I walk to a new spot and try to remember you, but it's been getting harder. As the number of sunsets between your funeral and now become double, then triple digits, I feel as though I cannot see the corners of your face anymore. I try to remember the roundness of your cheeks, the roundness of all of you. You and I were always the fat ones, united by the soft, white rolls of our bodies, our ancestry of largeness. Our family called us luxuriant food nicknames that tasted bitter when shouted at us: fatty pork, chicken skin, pork belly, roast piglet. We got the fat from our fathers—short, wobbly, roll-ridden men without much purpose whom our mothers grew to detest, though their hatred manifested in different ways: mine left and remarried my stepfather, a thin, angry man who also left her within a few years, while yours stayed and complained bitterly about it every day until the bitterness engulfed her body and killed her with its cancer.

You moved into our house when your father locked you and your mother out of the shophouse you used to live in. It stormed that day. I remember because you and your mother were drenched when you arrived, she hitting you relentlessly with a flipped-over pink umbrella. It's your fault, it's your fault, you slut, walking around with no clothes around your father, she screamed. I marveled at how you did not cry, just let her smack you as you walked into our house, her shouts so loud she could be heard over the thundering rain. My mother was uncharacteristically kind to you that day. She made you a bowl of herbal soup that she spooned into your mouth with a tenderness I had never seen.

We enrolled in primary school and cried when we were separated into different classrooms. Our teachers, weary of our sweat and tears, relented and let us enter Miss Kumar's class together. Other girls would make fun of us, call us fatty bom bom and smelly puki. I would lower my head and try to keep walking, tugging at your sleeve. But you would march up to the gaggle of thin, long-haired girls, push at them, stare them down. Sometimes they all pushed back, slamming you against the wall as they shouted those rude names, their young voices almost a harmonized chorus. I tried to step forward once, but you caught my eye and shook your head. I'll handle it, your eyes said. I got you.

Your father came by our house a few times over the years. Your mother would wear her finest cheongsam, a green and yellow silken confection that was so beautiful it made me hungry. She would spritz awful-smelling scents on herself that made me sneeze. Then our mothers would force us into identical blue dresses that had a layer of tulle under the skirt. The dresses were so itchy they left red welts on our thighs that we would rub ice on after. We would walk out of the house to the backyard sweating and trying not to scratch, where your father would sit on a long bench with your mother in a chair front of him, and the two of us flanked on his either side. My mother would watch through the window, eyes both hopeful and frightened. I wonder if she saw how your father wedged his hands under our skirts, pressed his fingers against the soft inner parts of our thighs, his calluses leaving bruises that we would later trace and map to the shapes of countries in our atlas. Yours looks like Australia, you said once, admiring the blue and red swirls on my thighs. And you have Mexico, I trilled, mesmerized by the thin purple curl on the end of your bruise. Your father's visits trailed off as your mother became thinner and thinner, the cheongsam that once hugged her tightly now dangling off her pronounced shoulders. The visits finally stopped when your mother became bald and bedridden, shouting and waving her hands at imaginary ghosts, her hallucinations her only comfort in the weeks before she finally succumbed.

I try in my dreams to touch you, to recall how you feel, but then I remember that it has been years since I have touched you. We touched constantly as children, hands held in sweaty communion as we ran around together. Even as we grew into ourselves, we would strip naked and inspect each other's changing bodies—your nipples darkening before mine, my vulva drooping lower than yours. But I also spent a lot of time watching you. I studied the side of your eye as it crinkled when I told you a joke as we walked to school, the side of your cheek as you sucked it in when you were angry or about to laugh really hard, the side of your arm that would tense whenever someone who wasn't me put their arm around you. I became an expert on the whole of your left side—the side I would always stand on when we were together, the side of the bed that I lay on when we were kids, on our pilled Little Miss bedsheets.

The day everything changed was the day you told me you were in love. We were fifteen, and to me it felt way too early. It's true that we were beginning to sneak out of school sporadically to meet with boys—in the playground, behind the sundry store, in the windy alley between the municipal building and the library. I would keep watch for you at these engagements which were always the same: a moaning boy, his khaki school uniform pants tangled around his ankles, his eyes rolling and his arms reaching for imaginary objects in the air as he tried to keep his balance, your mouth around his penis. It never lasted very long. He would buck, nearly losing his balance, then pull himself out from your lips, a string of saliva and cum linking you both until it broke off when the boy pulled up his pants and ran away. You always positioned me within your sight so we would lock eyes as you bounced your head back and forth, back and forth, lips puckered against the length of him. It was as though if we blocked out the boy's groans and shudders, it was just the two of us watching each other, our bodies aching, wet and ripe as fruit.

But then, the declaration of love. You told me it had been hard keeping the secret, especially from me, but he had told you that you had to. You told me that for the last few weeks, every night as I drifted off to sleep after our long chats, you would creep out of the bed we still shared and go see your father. You knew it was wrong, you said, but you felt drawn to him in a way that shocked your body, and no matter how you tried to exorcise him with other boys, he filled your thoughts, made you tingle, made you feel like you would explode if you could not be with him. I was devastated, not by the clear and absolute wrongness of everything, but by the fact that all the while I had watched you with the boys in the alleys, my body's desire leaking down the side of my leg, you had been thinking of him—your father—who had the same jiggling body as we did, who bruised us, who I thought had finally gone away.

When did he come back, I asked.

He came back one day when you and your mother were at the market. When he walked in, it felt like magnets attached to his and my chest and pulled us together. When he hugged me, I thought I would burst into fire, you sighed.

Flames, I thought spitefully, the expression is burst into flames. I was wracked with jealousy, my own body hot and red and itchy. How dare he encroach on the lives we had built together, how dare he make you keep a secret from me, how dare he take you when you were mine.

For days after you told me I avoided you, slept at the furthest corner of our bed although that wasn't far since it was a single bed. I refused to speak to you, refused to meet your eye at mealtimes, crossed the road and walked on the opposite side staring straight ahead when we walked to school. Your sadness became fear. Are you going to tell your mother, you asked me over and over again. I'll do anything for you, please, please don't, you begged, holding my limp fingers in yours. I said nothing back to you, but I also said nothing to anyone else because despite everything, when I imagined you and him together—your mouth wrapped around your father's penis—it soaked me, made me want you even more, and that disgust made me so nauseous I barely ate.

Eventually I asked my mother if I could clear out the storeroom in the house and move in there. We're growing up, I said, I think we need separate rooms. You watched soundlessly as I packed up my meager belongings and kicked them over to the storeroom on the other side of the hall. I also began to spend more time at the houses of other girls from our class, staying there all day after school so I could avoid you. At dinner, my mother tried to engage us in conversation. How was your day, what did you do, girls, she would ask, but we would just mutter unintelligibly and refuse to meet each other's eyes.

We even stopped looking alike. You stayed the same round shape, but I became lithe and thin. In a way my self-loathing helped. Every time I needed to throw up my meal, I thought about you and a boy in the alley, or if that didn't work, you and your father, but mostly just you-you-you. As aching desire filled the area above my pelvis, my disgust would overwhelm me, and my stomach would empty itself. My body and I quickly became the envy of the neighborhood. Boys would whistle as I passed, and I would see you standing some distance away, your eyes unreadable, your white school shirt stretched against your stomach and shining with sweat.

Sometime midway during Form 5, about seven months before our general examination, I came home to find you wailing on the floor, your cheeks pressed into the gray kitchen tile, the grout leaving an indentation on your cheek.

What the fuck, I said, the first time I had directly addressed you in nearly two years.

He's getting married, you screamed between hysterical sobs. He's going to leave me.

I dragged you to your bed, pausing as the scent of you from your room wafted over me. I hadn't so much as glanced in there since I moved into the storeroom, and it looked exactly the same. I sat on the Little Miss sheets that pilled and crinkled on the edges; you were never good at making the bed. As you cried, I learned that your father was going to be marrying one of his office girls, the prettiest one who brought him tea every day, even when you were around.

She was attractive, you said, but older than you, at least twenty-something, so you were never worried. You had planned for you and your father to move out of town after our general examination. People wouldn't understand here, but elsewhere, maybe they would, and you and he wouldn't have to be a secret.

I marveled at how childlike you were, wondered how we were only six months apart in age. No one would understand *anywhere*, I said. It's just wrong. He forced you.

He! Did! Not! You were indignant, actually stopping your weeping to glare at me. I found myself caught in my reflection in the dark, wet pools of your eyes. Then you screamed at me.

You've always been jealous. You've never understood. You don't know what love is like.

My heart ached. But I do, I thought.

You rose from the bed, leaving a divot on Little Miss Sunshine's face. As you walked away, I watched the sweat stain on the back of your school uniform skirt get smaller and smaller, leaving me sitting on the Little Miss sheets, my hands wet with your tears.

Perhaps it was inevitable, your death. My mother said it was an accident, that you had simply not looked where you were going and crossed the tracks into the moving KTM train, but I knew better. You killed yourself the day before your father's wedding, a week after

I turned seventeen. His distress gave him a stroke, and his young wife-to-be, horrified by the sight of your father's drooping, stroke-addled face, left him.

Two months after your funeral, desperate to keep your memories alive, I begin swallowing you. Well, not you exactly, but the things that remind me of you. I tip the ink from those glittery pens down my throat, choke as the thick bitterness clots its way down my esophagus. I imagine the glitter coloring my small intestine purple. I chew up your favorite stamps, the plain, ugly ones of paddy fields that everyone has. I bought you specialty stamps once, with faces of Malaysia's former prime ministers on them, but you rolled your eyes and said that you would never lick the back of a corrupt leader, even in stamp form. I press the sand from the playground where we met boys onto my tongue; bite down on the gritty bits and swallow a large gulp of water to wash it down. I even take a trip to the Petronas gas station where you had your explosive shit. I crouch at the bowl and drop a little bit of toilet water on my tongue. It doesn't taste like much, but the smell of the toilet makes me gag, so I take the opportunity to throw up my lunch.

Sometimes these swallowing escapades upset my stomach. When I swallow the glitter pen ink, I shit purple for days, and when I wipe my ass, streaks of shimmer dot the brown. The gas station water gives me sharp stomach pains, but because I barely eat, I am unable to get relief. Still, these episodes please me because it feels like I can sense you again. Even if I am losing your face, ingesting bits of your life makes me feel like you are, just for a moment, with me.

Finally, I think I am ready. In November, I sit for the general examination. Every day for two weeks, me and five hundred other girls in my class crouch over our desks, shading in answers in multiple-choice test sheets, filling blue book after blue book with essays. I am focused, more focused than I have ever been, with mental clarity I have not had in years, not since I walked out of our shared bedroom and built a life separate from yours. The day of my final paper, I walk out of the school and inhale deeply, pushing the warm afternoon air down my throat. It is time.

We're going to Pizza Hut, some of the girls from school yell. Come with! I shake my head no, I have something else I need to take care of. I cross the tracks and hop on the KTM train. I wonder if it's the same one that hit you; if they simply wiped you off the front and reintegrated the train into the schedule. I hug my school bag close to me and run over my plan in my head. I am pleased; there are no gaps, it is neat and precise.

The next town over, I hop off. Although the nursing home is only ten minutes away, it's midday and the sweltering Malaysian heat sticks my school bag to my back. Sweat drips off me but it also smells like your sweat, and the familiarity takes my breath away. At the nursing home, the security guard barely looks up as I sign in. I had prepared a whole speech. I'm visiting my father, I had planned to say. I love him very much. I am almost disappointed at not having to use it.

I pause outside your father's room and press my ear against the door. I hear the rattling sound of an old man breathing and push the door open. Your father is lying on the bed, propped up by pillows. He is watching *Sesame Street* on television, his mouth agape, one side of his face sunken from Bell's palsy, a leftover effect from the stroke. He claps as the children on screen laugh, licks his lips as they begin to sing. When he sees me, his eyes light up. Then he says your name.

"Dorinda," he cries, his voice high and shaky.

Whether he recognizes me or not, will not make a difference.

"Yes, Papa, I'm here," I murmur. I unpack the contents of my school bag—raffia string to tie his hands, a ball of socks to muffle his mouth, a bandana to blindfold him. But now, seeing how frail he is, I put them all away. I won't need any of my planned implements.

I crawl into bed on top of him, wrinkling my nose at the stale smell of sweat and urine that coats the air around his body. I turn off the TV. I pull the thin sheet off him and his eyes dance. "Dorinda," he groans. "I've missed you."

I take him in my mouth, limp and covered in excess skin, and get to work. Back and forth, back and forth as I had seen you do in the alleys. "Thank you, my girl," he murmurs. "My girl, my best girl." My jaw aches. I worry he will never get hard. But eventually I feel him swell, poking against my gums. A little bit of liquid drips off the tip into my mouth, precum or pee, I cannot tell. I swallow deeply and will myself not to choke. "You know how I like it, Dorinda, yes my girl," he cries and I want so badly to bite down and taste his blood, but I do not. Instead I pull my mouth off him and swap in my hand. I lie the full length of me on top of his body as I move my hand up-up-down, up-up-down. His eyes flutter close, "Uh, uh, Dorinda, uh," he moans. When I wrap my hands around his neck, he opens his eyes, first in surprise, then excitement. "Oh Dorinda, you've learned a few things," he says. But when I tighten my hands into fists around both his neck and his penis, his eyes get large, then roll to the back of his head, the sunken side of his face quivering.

I wonder if you are watching, and the thought turns me on a little. I tighten my grip. Your father chokes and kicks his legs feebly under me. I feel a warm wet gush over my hand, and the hiss of his last breath snakes through his mouth. I squeeze my fingers around his neck once more for good measure.

When I take my hands off him and wipe them on the bed, I see the beginnings of a bruise forming around his neck. It looks like the map of Japan. I make a note to check our atlas.

AQUAFINA

CHANA PORTER

1.

Girl, you are a water bottle
and also a stone cold B

You ran out into the desert to find yourself
you duplicated yourself to build houses

you carried yourself to the landfill to rest
you brought yourself to the party
and other people collected you, afterwards
collected you and traded you in
for small sums of money

you made yourself an evil
that only felt necessary

I don't know how to love you,
Aquafina
but I want to.

2.

Aquafina is prettier than me
If I had a boyfriend he would have a crush on Aquafina
I don't have a boyfriend

A says I should be glad because
that means I'm free to live life
but actually I don't want to live life
I want someone to play with my hair while we watch TV

Wherever we go, heads turn
I have always suspected
the alternate reality of very beautiful women
but now I know
it is real.

When I am with Aquafina,
we get free stuff all the time
drinks, meals, parking
once a man ran out of a store to give her a cashmere sweater
She said Thank You so calmly
like she'd been expecting a delivery.

I like these kinds of gifts best
from the men who do not expect anything from us
they are petitioners at the temple of her beauty
paying homage

Right now we are driving a free upgrade
from the car rental

drinking free iced lattes
in the late morning sun.

There are other men
who see Aquafina's beauty
as a natural resource to be exploited
a demand made upon them

They make jokes, they give us their room keys
they insert themselves between us and the elevator door until we
smile

Some say all streams lead to the ocean
and that's where we're going
I've never seen the Pacific
I've never seen San Francisco
I've never climbed a mountain
but with you all things feel possible
Aquafina

Do you think another world is possible?

3.

You are good and you are bad
I am good and I am bad

You stole milk from mothers
then packaged it up to sell back to them
for a price they could not
not afford

Double negative, Aquafina
but haven't we all.

I am critical of myself
but only in flashes
like catching traces of lightning
in the summer sky

4.

Aquafina and I are on a road trip
and I'm trying to have fun but she's making it really difficult
I changed the song on the radio

and she sighed at me like
and I said What
and she said What
and I said What
and then there was a really long pause
and then she said You're afraid of money.

And we didn't talk for the rest of the day
just drove and drove hundreds of miles in silence
and then she fell asleep
She looked so pretty in profile
like an angel or a model or someone from daytime TV

While Aquafina was sleeping
I composed letters in my head to my ex-boyfriend
I'm sorry I'm too porous

like a frog, I could write
because I heard that frogs are very porous
and that's why pollution is so bad for them
I'm sorry I have bad boundaries
I see that now and I'm working on it
I shouldn't have slept with you after we broke up
That was confusing for you
I shouldn't have gotten back together with you
after that night where you yelled at me for two hours
or gone with you to that wedding
and met all your friends from college
who pitied me.

When Aquafina woke up night had fallen
and she was suddenly nice again
bubbly, overflowing
my best friend Aquafina
like our little fight never happened.

She had just been cranky
hungry or tired or thirsty
and discovering this little detail made me happy
like we had a secret

Aquafina looked out the window with her vast ocean eyes
the desert a sea of sand
Then she spoke brightly, practically chirping,
continuing our last conversation
as if she had never fallen asleep

You're afraid of money, she said.

Afraid of everything about it.
You're afraid to be poor,
afraid to struggle,
afraid to pinch to make ends meet
afraid to say No or I can't,
afraid to be surprised
by a broken fan belt a broken carburetor a broken tooth a broken
leg
But just as much or maybe more
you're afraid to have money
afraid it will make you sick and weak
a healthy woman always getting colonics
wanting money to clean you from the inside out

You want to be kept safe
without ever having to make any real choices
and that's why you're a coward.

And then she changed the radio
and
we spoke of other things

Las Vegas shimmered into view
glimmering and wide
like a swimming pool at night.

5.

Aquafina, how do I recuse you?
We turned around once to see the land filled

but we titans of industry
we built a park on top of those old immediacies
and opened up a coffee shop.

You are so positive!
I really like that about you
You make me feel like everything will always be good
but also better.

You make me feel like the world is so big
because you are so small
how could there ever not be room enough for us?
how could there ever not be room enough for me?

The hotel was really fancy so they gave out Aquafina
for free

6.

When Aquafina asked me if I wanted to go on a road trip
I said Yes without thinking

I want to discover America
I want to look pretty pumping gas
I want to drink coffee at a roadside diner while the sun spreads low

Close up on me sharing a slice of apple pie
with my best friend Aquafina

I have never seen Aquafina eat

but I'm excited to be near her
and learn her secret
protein powder or Ensure
four small bowls of just brown rice
only broth and green juice 'til five
She's probably a raw vegan or perhaps
she's learned how to ingest sunshine

They say real women have curves
but Aquafina contains her own precise architecture.
She doesn't need to diet.
She doesn't need to floss
or bleach
or straighten.
She doesn't need three weird tricks to flatten her stomach.
She isn't trying to find her beach body in time for summer.
Aquafina is one long season.
A didn't glow up, didn't grow up.
She emerged from a seashell, whole,
to conquer me.

Every time I am hungry I drink more water.
Bottles and bottles of purified water.
I am becoming purified.
It makes me have to pee.
We're off to look for America,
with scarves tied around our heads.
Like Thelma and Louise,
except we won't die.

7.

Aquafina, do *you* think that you are good?
I am just beginning to learn how to love
it's not your fault I was abusive

Carrying clean water is good!
Here are some other ways to be good:

good looking
a good employee
a good partner
good in bed
good with numbers
a good drinker
a good driver
a good parent
a good baby
a good friend
a good listener
a good student
a good steward

Be good to yourself
eat clean
get plenty of sleep
and oh yeah
drink lots of water.

8.

In Las Vegas
we were bored so we pretended we were prostitutes
and let two businessmen fuck us
you got the handsome one
but mine wasn't bad-looking
cute, I would have done it for free, gladly
in my new dress and my shaved legs
and my discount designer heels and my handbag
which is a very expensive fake
But you were right, Aquafina
it was fun to pretend to be call girls
when we did it I was so excited
I couldn't help but get so wet
I was a river and you were removed
looming above us, like you were on the ceiling
a queen and her subjects down in the dirt
No one touches you, Aquafina
even when they're inside you
and I understand that now
when we were backdown on the bed
legs open, strangers moving over us
our heads touching
you were far away

because you have realized the secret to bodies
which is that we don't really have them.

9.

I love swimming.
I love submerging myself in water
I love diving into lakes and splashing in the ocean
I love swimming naked
it feels absurdly human
I love showering with my boyfriend
I love showering with your boyfriend
I love hot tubs
I love swimming pools
I love bathhouses
I love Korean spas
I worship water
and I love you.

Aquafina, when I was little I wanted to be a mermaid
what did you want to be when you grew up?
a bicycle?
an organ donor?
a fresh piece of fruit?
the whole sky?

Does water have desires?

I drank a bottle of water in the Uber back to my hotel
the long plane ride made me thirsty
even though I drank from so many little cups
I am separated out from the ocean in form but that is an illusion
I am big in my smallness
vast and near in my separation

10.

Afterward, Aquafina took a bath
while I looked at my phone and counted our new money.

She takes long baths and showers every day.
I think this might be a secret to her beauty.
She needs to be watered, like a plant.

11.

Aquafina, do you think in the future there will be more or less of
you?
Is that a rude question?

On my phone
I read that the ice caps are melting and
at the border
guards destroy
the jugs of water
left out
for migrants
under the omniscient sun.

12.

The next morning I was still wet
in my velour sweatpants
I was giddy, in love with myself

in love with you, with us, Aquafina
with how dangerous and sexy and unpredictable we are together
like rain in the desert.

You looked at me
over the chipped mugs of dishwater coffee
my queen of the diner
my priestess of Route 66
you smiled at me to punch me in the gut
just like you meant to
And you said, Sweetie
you never pretend to be anything
you just are.

The words you spoke but didn't speak
just hung there
like clothes on a wire
And then you said
Never give away what you had to pay for
every day of your life
every day of your life
with your own blood

I loved you then
more than I loved even my own name
Aquafina
I didn't ask any more questions
or try to share a story from my childhood
about an uncle who or
a trusted neighbor that or
the boyfriend who cut me and ran.

I said nothing,
but the words swirled around us like mist

lies are free
the truth is for sale
money is free
trust is for sale
sex is free
love is for sale
water is free
godliness is for sale

Aquafina Aquafina Aquafina Aquafina
I am talking to myself again

13.

I'll be your whore again
if you hold my hand while we do it

14.

One day I'll forget about you
forget the exact color of your eyes
the fuzz on your cheek like a peach
your slender toes
your hollow bones
Aquafina
I'll cannibalize you til I don't need you anymore

15.

The next time, Aquafina kept her dress on.
She lit a cigarette and stepped back to consider us
like a director.

This is my sister, she said.
Her name is Ocean.
She hasn't been with many men.
She is very special.
I'm going to show you how to fuck her.

16.

We left Vegas without a backward glance
while the businessmen turned to salt
off into the sunset
where all road trip movies end

in California

I was coming home to a person I have never been
in California
a sunshine girl
who gets beach waves
and breast implants

We didn't drive to the beach
we didn't drive to Hollywood
we didn't drive to the Sunset Strip

We drove to a benign suburb
still within the long arm of Los Angeles
The palm trees were green
and the air smelled like something you could eat
there is a future here, I thought
as Aquafina got out of the car.
I waited in the driveway
while she knocked on the door
of a small, white house.

Her mother was there in the threshold
she was also made of water

17.

Aquafina's mother is a smoker who no longer smokes
they catch up at the kitchen table
by recounting everyone who now has illnesses
I drink wine from a box
the sun is setting in California

In the kitchen
Aquafina's mother tells her that the boy who raped her
now has cancer
and it's not looking good
the air is shiny with unspoken words

Her mother said
Well, if I looked at every bad date like some kind of rape

18.

For a split second I am Aquafina's mother
I want to touch her but my hands don't remember how
I am a smoker who no longer smokes
I am a drinker of diet iced tea
I say, if every bad date was some kind of rape
Well, I don't know where that would leave me
Well
at the bottom of a well
I guess
starving and wet.

19.

A child falls into the well and no one hears her
A child falls into the well and I am more than my body
A child falls into the well and well?

20.

Upon blinking, I am disappointed to discover that her mother is
my mother. All of the pictures, all over the house, are of me—my
first communion, my bat mitzvah, my confirmation, all the mile-
stones bear my face. My mother fills a bag of oranges, picked from a
tree in the yard. She hands it to me for the ride and then the vision
is gone. I am me and Aquafina is next to me, her mother is touching her hair, telling her to be safe, to call, to come back soon. I scan
the small house and try to bring myself back there. I do not come.

21.

Aquafina I'll forget all of this
maybe one day soon
like the summer I forgot my own name
like the winter I forgot my own face

22.

We the blood of dinosaurs, we the ancient
we the processed, remade in an image
something to be filled up with something else
Aquafina, I'm putting my shoulder to the wheel

23.

We get back in the car
and drive to the beach
The sun has set
the sky is pregnant with the moon

I look at where the water meets the sky
suspended in moonlight gleaming down
I resist the urge to howl

Aquafina howls
she howls and howls until she cries
then she laughs
and suddenly it's like I'm in a movie

and she's the main character and I'm the fucking friend
I'm always the fucking friend
even in my own life
And this makes me angry
and my anger makes me powerful
makes me beautiful
So I take off all my clothes
and run into the waves

The water is cold and dark
and salty with life
Something reedy brushes my leg
I turn around to see Aquafina
naked behind me
grinning like a jackal
under that full-bellied moon

She says
I'm so glad you came with me.
I couldn't do this without you.

The night
and the cold
and the saltwater
and her love
make me brave

I say
I love you and I hate you
I say
I want you

and I want to be you.

When she looks at me,
her eyes are soft with surprise

I can't really love anybody,
she says gently.
Because I'm a water bottle.

I carry her back to the car
I always forget how light she is
She looms so large in my imagination
but I could fit her in my purse.

24.

If I was a beautiful object I would never die
If I was a beautiful object I would never grow old
If I was carved from plastic I would always be plastic

25.

We get back in the car
and drive to the beach

Our feet are still covered in falling ashes,
from when we realized we were one person
and blew up that big building downtown.

26.

We get back in the car
and drive to the beach

Our hands and faces are still streaked with blood,
from when we put the brick in the bag
and bashed her mother's head in,
left her
bleeding out
on the linoleum floor.

27.

We get back in the car
and drive to the beach

Our hands are still trembling
from when we clasped them together
and drove off that desert cliff.

28.

We get back in the car
and drive to the beach

The water washes off the blood, the ashes
the water makes us new.

We can be whatever we want in the ocean,
without those old stories chaining us to other histories.

29.

I turn around to see
Aquafina naked behind me
grinning like a jackal

She says
I'm so glad you came with me.
She says
I couldn't do this without you.

There is night between us.
There are stars below us.
There is sea above us.
There is water inside us.

State lines
criss cross
the lines on my arms,
the pale of her legs, long,
extending out like an open road.

My body is a place I sometimes visit
Maybe I could even live there
If I had a map,
if there was an X to the mark the spot

She closes the gap between us
then pauses in front of my eyes like a stop sign
Her mouth is a mirror of my mouth
We open and close together

Then the sea is a blanket,
her hair is the sheets,
the word for world is water
and for once in my life I am not afraid.

That is a lie.
I am afraid.

but I don't mind.

If I drown in her ocean
it is because
I had only just learned breathing
If I drown in her ocean
it is because I was dead long ago

If I drown in this ocean
tell my mother I'm still angry

If I drown in this ocean
tell my body it's okay to rest.

30.

Aquafina struggles with drowning.

Plastic resists sinking,
and girl wants to float.

But I show her how.

I sink down,
let the cold swallow me whole.
The fluid fills my lungs
feel my insides twitch and gather,
the change is total, rapidly complete
The land is no longer my home
My legs, a problem my whole life,
thighs too skinny or too fat,
hips too wide or butt too flat,
they merge and dissolve
into my thick, muscular tail.

Cautious at first,
we keep close to the shoreline
drinking in the nourishing cold through our pores

As we travel
further and further afield,
we find other mermaids.

They have always been here.
They nod to us as we swim on.

A SCHOLARSHIP OPPORTUNITY

MEGAN GIDDINGS

Worst Girl Question #1: What is the true essence of being the worst?

Tiffani is in genuine contention for being the worst, at least according to her family, her teachers, some of her friends. Her mother often says, with great annoyance, great affection, great anger, "Tiffani is the worst girl to be born into this family, filled with terrible girls, for at least five generations." *You dumbass*, Tiffani thinks whenever her mom says this. Tiffani knows that a) all the family records were destroyed when the septic tank in her grandmother's basement became some sort of incomprehensible poop volcano, so there is no proof now that T is the worst of them and b) she has heard Aunt Retta call her daughter, Tiffani's cousin, the actual worst girl in the family. And that cousin did once have to do community service for sprayprainting the words Dumb Bitch High on the sidewalk outside her high school. And c) if Tiffani is truly that bad, why won't her mother let her actually prove it?

Worst Teen Girl in America comes with a full-ride scholarship and even some cash and therapy vouchers for the winner. Tiffani knows it would look good on her CV when applying for colleges next year. It would soften the blow of being a girl who has been banned from all beauty supply chains in a fifty-mile radius for shoplifting, heckling the makeup artists about their love of contouring, and for once saying that blowout culture is white supremacy and getting three different white ladies to leave the store mid-blowout.

Why do you have to embarrass us, Tiffani? her mother asks when Tiffani shows her the brochure for the first time, the second time, the fifth time.

Things that Tiffani's mom seems to find embarrassing about her: her B- in geometry, *how can you not understand shapes,* Tiffani's disinterest in driving, *you're not going to be cute forever, only cute people get rides whenever they ask,* Tiffani's butt, *when I was your age, I was much thinner,* when Tiffani is clearly thinking rude things, *you're making a very unpleasant face, Tiffani, it'll freeze that way,* Tiffani sneaking out of the house to make out with people in their cheap SUVs, the thrill of moonlight sucking its gray teeth at her through the window as she dips her tongue into a desperate mouth, *Tiffani, can't you at least say you're in love instead of saying you're having fun?* Tiffani's current life goals of either being a philosopher or owning a movie theater, *Tiffani, I cannot give you money forever.*

WORST GIRL QUESTION #2: WHAT IS THE WORST THING YOU EVER THOUGHT ABOUT YOUR MOTHER? BE SPECIFIC.

"I just want to go to college," Tiffani replies each time. On its cover are three girls who are not smiling, but they are wearing crowns with their arms crossed. They were photoshopped to be standing on the words ALL YOUR COLLEGE PAID.

Her parents do want her to go to college, but they would like to have a firm grip on the map of her life. Tiffani's dad has said some vague things about going to college to meet a better sort of people.

She thinks this means he would like her to meet a nice boy who likes his parents and hopefully the parents of that boy she likes will maybe have some money and find Tiffani kinda sorta okay. Tiffani's mother wants her to be a lawyer or a doctor.

Tiffani knows that on some level, college is inherently a scam. You spend thousands and thousands of dollars and some of the teachers have never actually learned how to teach. You spend thousands and thousands of dollars only to skip class because you drank too much beer trying to impress a dipshit who thinks good hygiene is to spray on some Axe after going to the gym. You spend thousands and thousands of dollars to get a degree in Communications where you write papers about interpersonal relationships; meanwhile, the only real way you can talk to people is after sitting in a blunt circle and inhaling enough OG Hulkmania to blurt out a compliment or two. But wasn't being at home with your parents an even bigger scam? Wasn't letting them choose the rest of your life potentially the worst idea ever?

For the first time, her mother does not walk away or return to her phone. "What if you did an actual beauty pageant? Or wrote an essay?"

"Why not all of them?"

"I just want you to have a comfortable life," her mom says. "I'm tired already of having to worry about you."

"I love you, too," Tiffani rolls her eyes.

Her mother looks at her face. Tiffani doesn't blink or look away against the assessment. A popped whitehead on her chin, but everywhere else is mostly clear for once. The skin light brown and even. The unplucked, unshaped eyebrows. Her chapped lips. Her fingernails painted black. Her long legs in the black shorts that her vice principal said were "entirely inappropriate for learning." Tiffani got detention for calling the vice-principal "a gender fascist who is more concerned with immature young men than a woman's right to education." Her mother had said that wasn't wrong, but maybe Tiffani could find a better, more helpful way to express her views.

"You are the worst girl to be born into this family for five generations," her mother says. "Good luck."

WORST GIRL QUESTION #3: WHY DO YOU DISOBEY YOUR PARENTS?

In the car her parents refused to lend her, Tiffani applies soft pink lipstick. She has put her hair into an approximation of a mohawk: slicked tight to the sides, all combed and up in the middle for a burst of wild curls. It took hours of watching a YouTube tutorial from a spooky-voiced Black girl from the UK who kept saying, "Blacks are the original goths." "Sure, sis," Tiffani said after the third time the YouTube girl said it, and she put the video on mute. It took a lot of potential outfits, but Tiffani is dressed in unflattering chinos and a light blue polo shirt pulled tight against her chest. She knows that looking like someone who is grumpily being asked to conform is important. It'll make her look simultaneously sexy and up to no good.

"I don't know," Tiffani mutters to herself.

At the heart of everything, even having to do something like this is a disappointment. She is glad that she's taking her future into her own hands. But the rage Tiffani feels even now, not yet eighteen, that she has to choose to lean into other people's judgments? It's so deeply unfair. To be a bad man, you have to do such over-the-top shit that people feel actually comfortable talking about you. But money and height and hair and a deep voice can cushion you toward neutrality. It feels unfair, and Tiffani feels like this is a weed thought without the weed—she is coming into this pageant sharp—that there is no such thing as neutrality for anyone who isn't a cis white man. Her parents told her to stop saying cis, it makes her sound like a nut on the news.

"It's not a slur, dummies," Tiffani had said back, and that's why she has technically stolen the car because her parents took away car privileges for two weeks.

She sprays on perfume that stinks of roses. She pulls out a cigarette from her bag and lights it in the air. Tiffani doesn't smoke cigarettes. They make her too wired and give her a head cold. But all perfumes smell better when mixed with cigarette smell.

"College, college, college," Tiffani says and gets out and walks to the auditorium. "Freedom, freedom, freedom."

She would like to turn around, drive ninety miles an hour, and ask her mother, "Why can't you just try to understand me?"

It's the question that's been living in her mouth since she was six years old.

The auditorium is filled with girls that look just like Tiffani. Wearing pink peony pajama sets, prom dresses that look like overdecorated cupcakes, tuxedos, mechanic-style jumpsuits, slip dresses, and one in a bat onesie, the wings drifting down her sides, the ears pointed up. Hair buzzed, hair chemically straightened like T's mom always wanted her to do because it'll look "professional," natural hair, a few wearing cheap-summer-popsicle bright wigs. Their voices are all the same and the sound of herself mixing into one extra loud voice, it aches.

WORST GIRL QUESTION #4: WHY DON'T YOU CARE ABOUT WHAT
OTHER PEOPLE THINK?

All of them turn and say, "Tiffani!" and then start laughing.

Our laugh is awful, Tiffani thinks.

A woman strides out wearing a headset and big glasses and holding a clipboard. "Your name?"

"Tiffani."

"A popular one today." The woman's voice sounds like she's telling a joke that Tiffani missed the setup for.

She gives Tiffani the run of show. They will parade in a circle. Answer questions. They will do a talent. Answer more questions. She hands Tiffani a form to sign. The woman doesn't ask about her parents or getting their approval and it makes Tiffani's shoulders relax.

In the parade, all the Tiffanis walk in semi-darkness, pose in a spotlight, they say, "Hello, I am Tiffani Arnold and I am the worst girl in Grand Blanc, Michigan," and then walk backstage. When Tiffani makes it, she crosses her arms and says the same thing as everyone else and looks into the audience. It's filled with no one she can recognize. They clap appreciatively as if they have not heard the name Tiffani Arnold seventeen times before this iteration of it. There's a faint popcorn smell in the air, but no one is eating. The stage smells like sweating bodies and the processed-food scent of cheap cosmetics.

As Tiffani listens to all the other Tiffanis saying they are "the worst girl," she pauses to wonder what that truly means. What has she done in her life that was truly that bad? Why does everyone want her to conform so badly? She shakes off the thoughts. The time to consider those questions is late at night, alone in her bedroom with the quilt pulled over her head, not now when they could ruin everything.

Next, they're brought out in groups of five and asked to answer the same three questions, asked by a man that Tiffani thinks she recognizes from the local PBS affiliate. Do you believe that world peace is possible in your lifetime? What would you do with a full-ride to college? What would being made "the worst girl" mean to you?

Every Tiffani until our Tiffani answers the same way: World peace is impossible. I would get to do what I want. It would be proof that I am actually "the worst girl," and it would be nice to have that accomplishment before I even get to college. With each answer, the

crowd claps, some people make big, thoughtful hmmms. The sounds
are the same every time in a way that the longer Tiffani waits, the
more dread she feels.

When it's finally Tiffani's turn, the spotlight feels like actual sunshine after a winter's worth of weak light. She feels taller and more
alert. "I think world peace can only happen if people fight against
one of the world's greatest evils: self-centeredness." It is not an immediately popular answer but the people she can see near the front of
the stage are making big thinking faces.

"A full-ride to college means that I'll actually get a chance to
learn and maybe become the person I want to be." The polo shirt
feels scratchy. The heat from the lights is making her perfume feel extra loud against her nose. The people clap super hard for that answer.
Tiffani flushes.

"Being the worst girl means, at least, I'll be remembered. Whenever I go to history class, we learn about all of these men. And we're
not supposed to put any value on what they did. I got a C for complaining about that in an essay. But I'm only going to be here for, if
I'm lucky, maybe eighty years. I don't want to be a good mother or
a good wife. I want to be remembered for me, the things I do, the
way I approached the world. I don't think there's anything wrong
with wanting to be either of those things, mostly, but I want people
to actually know my name. And this would at least be a start in that
direction."

The crowd is a mixture of boos and applause. Tiffani thinks that's
for the best. The other Tiffanis are watching her, and she can tell
they're all uncomfortable with how honest she's being. Tiffani thanks
the audience and goes backstage.

None of the other Tiffanis look pleased to see her. Some of them
whisper to each other and laugh in a way that makes Tiffani squirm.
She vows to never do this to another person again, make them feel

the force of how derisive she can be. One of them bumps her and says, "Excuse me," as if it was Tiffani who bumped into her and was being insufferably rude. Another Tiffani shoves that one. Tulle and denim nip at her arms. Then another shoves her. Soon, they are all pushing and pulling at each other. All the other Tiffanis are saying, "Why can't you just be normal for once?" Tiffani yells, "I just want to like myself," and is so embarrassed by the honesty in what she has yelled, she doesn't even try to dodge when the closest Tiffani pulls her into a headlock. Another pulls out a handheld mirror that is cute with rabbit ears and a slender gold handle. She hits one Tiffani in the cheek with it—slap. Hits another on the forehead and the glass shatters.

The clipboard woman runs into the melee and says, "I'll disqualify all of you if you don't stop this instant." She is calm and Tiffani, despite being in the middle of having her frohawk pulled, is impressed by the poise. Most of the Tiffanis stop. One fishes a red Gatorade out of her tote bag, opens it, and pours it all over Clipboard's head.

"I win," says that Tiffani. "I'm the worst Tiffani."

"Get out," says Clipboard. "You're disqualified."

WORST GIRL QUESTION #5: HAVE YOU EVER DESTROYED SOMEONE ELSE TO FEEL A LITTLE BETTER ABOUT LIVING?

In the talent competition, the Tiffanis dance, they sing, one recites a poem by William Carlos Williams and is booed so thoroughly she runs out of the gymnasium and is never seen again. Tiffani, her hair looking even cooler from the fight, brings out a cardboard box and a bat. There is a long white table waiting for her. She opens the box and inside is a beautiful porcelain dinner set and tablecloth. Tiffani hums to herself as she spreads out the embroidered cloth, making it even and smooth. She sets four places. The dishes have a red rose and vine design. They're her mother's; a gift she has slowly been getting over many years from her mother-in-law. Places out gold flatware in the correct order. Wine glasses and water glasses. The audience is rapt as Tiffani folds napkins into rose swirls. She looks up while doing this, and her mother is there, in the front row, with an interested expression on her face.

She taught Tiffani how to do this before her mother's, Tiffani's grandmother's, funeral. They set up the luncheon together in silence. Tiffani's mother hadn't cried or done anything but listen to other people talk at her about her mother. She'd held a lot of hands, said a lot of kind things, and followed all the plans. There were bags under her eyes. Her shoulders shook. The lunch was going to be all of Grandma's favorite things: popcorn, baked ziti, chocolate shortbread, arugula with capers and a fussy vinaigrette, cheap white wine because it was too expensive to buy Sancerre for everyone. It was what she wanted. Tiffani watched as her mom folded napkin after napkin, creating a garden. "She loved making people feel welcome," her mother said, noticing the way Tiffani was watching. She showed Tiffani the folds, talked about the way it felt special to be able to do this, how annoying it was to feel obligated to do these welcoming little touches.

WORST GIRL QUESTION #6: WHAT IS THE LAST THING YOU STOLE FROM YOUR MOTHER?

"I would feel better about everything," her mother said, "if I could smash a plate every time someone asked me how I was holding up."

In the gymnasium, people are clapping at how beautiful the table is. And under the lights, it truly is. The plates glisten, the roses look extra red, and each place looks like it's waiting for someone to serve a special meal.

"Mom," Tiffani says, "can you come up here?"

Her mom nods. She springs up. The people applaud as she strides up to the stage. Tiffani says, "I know you've always wanted to do this."

Her mother smiles. She looks around. Tiffani follows her gaze. The crowd is filled now with Tiffani's mothers. Some of them are dressed just like her in her leggings, long shirt and soft wrap cardigan. They have their nails done. Their hair is straightened. A few are bald. One is wearing sunglasses and vaping and wearing an RIP Whitney shirt. Tiffani would like to sit next to that one. A few are wearing red lipstick. Some of them are crying. Most are tense and waiting to see what will happen next.

Tiffani offers her mother the bat.

"You are the worst girl in the world," her mother says and refuses the bat.

"I want you to understand me," Tiffani says.

Her mother opens her mouth and Tiffani knows her mother has stopped herself from saying, "I do understand you. You're my daughter." For once, she takes her daughter in. Tiffani meets her mother's eyes and offers the bat again.

Tiffani's mother breaks all the plates but one. Puts the bat down and, like a cat, goes through and slaps each glass off the table. The sound of them shattering is beautiful mixed in with Tiffani's applause. Some of the mothers cry, some laugh, a few cross their arms and clench their jaws. But her own mother is laughing. Joy that she so rarely lets out is spilling from her mouth, is smashing on the stage floor.

Her mother hands the bat back and points at the remaining dish. Tiffani lifts it and hits the plate's center. She doesn't think it matters now who wins. The plate shatters into six distinct pieces, each with its own rose. More beautiful in the break than when it was whole.

SICK

ALICIA ELLIOTT

T HERE ARE CERTAIN REALITIES that come along with being the oldest daughter to my mother. The most pressing one is that, according to her, I should be prepared at a moment's notice to give up whatever I'm doing so I can come back and cater to her needs. This is something that started when I was a child—this belief that I alone could soothe whatever ailed her, that I alone was responsible for her health and wellbeing, that this was my purpose: to serve and to save. This is something my therapist told me is called "parentification"— the expectation instilled in children that we should, essentially, parent our own parents. It was good to have a word for this, a way to explain this longstanding feeling that had oppressed me most of my life, even if the therapy that gave me this word was long enough ago that I no longer remembered how to actually stop myself from following those well-worn neural pathways of trauma back to my mother.

She had a car accident that had caused a spinal injury, she'd said. It would require someone to care for her for anywhere from three to six months. I'd asked my sister Carla if she would split the time with me, or even just go down one day a week so I could get a break, but she actually had the boundaries and the balls to say no.

Or, to be more accurate, she said, "Oh, fuck no. I'm not going back there. And you shouldn't, either. She'll railroad your whole life."

"Come on, Carla. She really needs us."

"She always needs us."

"Yeah, but for real this time. She has a doctor and nurses and a prognosis and everything. She needs the people who love her to take care of her."

"Did you actually talk to a doctor and confirm any of this?"

"That's the whole point of us being there. So we can figure things out with the doctors and nurses ourselves." I danced around the question—a skill I've seen my mother employ so often I've practically learned it via osmosis. But Carla knew those tricks, too.

"If she wanted either of us to be that kind of daughter, she should have been that kind of mother."

And then she hung up, not even momentarily considering that, despite all her talk about the importance of *my* boundaries and *my* life, she'd once again left the problem of our mother to me, taken away my ability to say anything other than a reluctant yet resounding "yes."

So, I pulled my teenage daughter Katie out of school practically kicking and screaming. She called me selfish over and over between furious tears as she tapped what were probably awful messages about me to her friends on her iPhone—the latest model, of course, which I'd preordered for her special even though I was months behind on credit card payments. And then I went to the manager of the discount grocery store I worked for and asked for a week of "leave" from my cashier job, claiming a nonexistent uncle died in another country and I needed to help organize everything, which was of course a lie, but a necessary one, I thought, since the store didn't offer leave any longer than that, and since it was easier and less shameful than telling my boss my mom was essentially making me quit so I could take care of her. And then I piled cheap, already-ripping garbage bags full of my daughter's and my clothes into our shitty car until it reeked of mildew and laundry detergent, and I headed home, resentment coursing through my blood, familiar as an old friend.

As soon as I was back inside her house I slid back into old habits and patterns like I slid into my oldest, most comfortable jeans. And as her criticisms and oversharing started to fill my ears, I smiled. I smiled and I smiled and I smiled, because if I didn't, I wasn't sure what I'd do. What I'd allow myself to do.

∽⊚∽

"Stop grinning like that. You're making me nervous," Mom says. She pulls up her big fleece blanket she got from the powwow to her chin, right over the black neck collar propping up her head, then folds it back precisely across her lap so it makes a perfect rectangle, the way she taught me to do whenever I made a bed. She spreads the fleece smooth, folds her hands, fingers perfectly tipped in a beige gel polish that hasn't chipped or grown out at all, despite her claims that her accident incapacitated her two weeks ago. Only after that does she turn her attention to me, my face, open and waiting like always. "Anyway, you smile too much. Wanna know how I know?"

"No," I huff too quietly, though that hardly matters. I know she's going to say it, regardless of whether I want to hear it or not.

"Because you're getting those nasty lines around your cheeks. I told you since you were a girl: only smile when you absolutely have to. If you don't control your face, wrinkles will take it over like weeds and then nobody will want you."

"Thanks a lot, Mom." I regret those words—their steely insolence—immediately. They aren't going to get what I want from the conversation. I try to focus on the laundry I'm variously folding to put away and setting aside to hang up. Mom's clothes are to be handled very specifically.

"Don't be like that. You know I'd buy you Botox injections if I had the money. Char, you know, over from church?" she asks. I don't say anything. Don't have to. "She set me up with her plastic surgeon and he gave me a discount. Nicest guy. Roger Berkley. Already married, of course he is, and putting his kids through university. One's in medical school, can you believe that? Like father, like son, I guess. They look a lot alike, actually. He's in a serious relationship, too, the son. I checked for you, just in case. Anyway, I got a gift pack of Botox treatments for myself for Christmas. You know, as a little treat. They're not transferable, otherwise I'd give you one. But since I can't…"

She shrugs with exaggeration, her arms floating back down onto her blanket as she avoids my eyes. That has always been one of her tells, that shrug. She's lying, naturally, and over something I couldn't give two shits about, also naturally. The ease with which she lies, the charm she somehow stamps onto it, even when she's lying about the most inconsequential thing in the world, like her favorite brand of smokes or what she ate for lunch, is probably why she's always fit in so well with her fellow Christians. The sins of her children—namely me—along with her string of live-in ex-boyfriends and questionable ex-husbands should probably have precluded her from their ranks. And yet, she's one of their most beloved members. When you lie so often and so well you wholeheartedly believe your own lies, as unable to parse the real from the fake as you would be to separate flour from already mixed dough, you know you have a talent you can sell.

And sell it my mother has. Her first supposed cancer diagnosis just so happened to coincide with my arrest at fourteen. Her fellow parishioners didn't have time to chastise my mother for raising a crazy, demonic child who'd nearly killed her only real friend when she herself was succumbing to cancer. An aggressive cancer that took all her precious, radiant hair in a matter of weeks after the crime, automatically making anyone who spoke ill of her into a monster. The fact that she was so beautiful before she lost her hair made the cancer that much more of a tragedy, at least aesthetically. And that was in many ways the point. Every time she appeared in photographs after that—my court appearances, in interviews with local and national media—she smiled in a sort of wounded way, her face always tilted downward, her eyes peeking up, her scarf-wrapped head the place your eyes went to first. *She's so sick*, the photos said. *How could she be to blame?* The discourse flipped immediately. It was no longer about what sort of parent could raise that aberration of a child; it was about what sort of evil child could do this to her mother, make her come to these courts and face these reporters, when she was so sick. She was the victim, again—of me, of Hope, of her own biology, of ancient, supernatural forces of evil that made me act the way I did. Even the devil was out to get her. Everything was a universe which rotated around her—especially me.

∽❧∽

I met Hope, ironically, through church. There was a group of about thirty kids, all preparing for our confirmations in the church basement. I was the only one who didn't go to the Catholic school attached to the church—Mom had pulled me from my public school for a few days specifically for this course—so once again I was the outsider. I was used to this. I was really only close to Carla, who everyone seemed to like, but who told me I couldn't talk to her at school because it embarrassed her.

The priest was showing us a video about some saint when one of the pretty girls, her smile sticky with lip gloss, leaned forward and complimented my brand-new shoes. They were Adidas Superstars Mom had given me the night before to help me make a good impression.

"Thanks," I'd said, shyly, embarrassing eagerness no doubt naked on my face.

And then the girl continued. They were nice...for obvious knockoffs. There were four lines on each side of the shoes instead of three. The guy sitting beside her, holding her hand, snickered. So did the other girls in her row.

I bit my lip 'til I tasted blood, panicked. Of course they were knockoffs. I was so stupid. For believing Mom. For not noticing.

And that's when Hope appeared beside me, like a spirit summoned to a séance.

"Fuck off, Courtney. You can't even suck your boyfriend's dick right. Or at least that's what Connor told me the other day." She turned to the boy beside Courtney, licking her lips with relish.

Hope dramatically leaned over to whisper to me, a hand in front of her mouth. "Now laugh really hard and give them all dirty looks."

I did exactly as she said. Courtney dropped Connor's hand and ran to the bathroom, him yipping after her, the word "slut" swirling in the air.

Hope had hit me like a lightning bolt. I was immediately bound to her after that. Later that night, on the phone, when I asked if she'd really sucked Connor's dick, she laughed. "Ew, no! I don't suck dicks that smell like vinegar."

I didn't ask how she knew his dick smelled like vinegar. She said these sorts of wild, intimate things so casually, so specifically, and only to me. It didn't even occur to me to think she was lying.

That's how it was when she started to tell me about what she called "lower demons" a few months later.

"Promise you won't think I'm crazy?" she asked.

"Oh, come on. Like I'd ever think that."

They came to her right as she was falling asleep, she said. They talked with her. Made her promises. Said they could make sure she and I became powerful and famous and rich, that they knew we wanted to leave our shitty families, and we could, but we'd have to sacrifice our most valuable thing first. As more details gushed from her lips every night—what the Devil was like (surprisingly reasonable), what demons really wanted (to deliver us from God and his twisted "salvation")—I gulped them down, unquestioned, considering: what was my most valuable thing?

The answer came immediately. My most valuable thing was her.

∽⦵∽

"You're so quiet," my mother says, her voice suspicious, and for a moment I wonder whether she can see into my head, the way I did when I was a kid. Her godlike refrain, *I know what you're thinking*, forever burned into my sinful mind. I can't even say the word "Hope" around her or she starts a fit.

"I was just thinking about your next appointment," I lie, turning from her to hang up her skirts, blouses and dresses.

"What about it, dear?" An edge to her voice under the sweet.

"I guess I don't understand why it's so far away. I mean, a back injury like yours—"

"SCI."

"Excuse me?" I ask, turning to face her.

"It's not technically called a back injury. It's called a spinal cord injury. Or SCI, for short." She smiles. "I don't expect you to *always* remember that, but if you can please try, I'd appreciate it. It's so important we use the proper terms for our injuries."

Proper terms for our injuries. I remember how she reacted when I tried to explain to her the proper term my therapist gave me for my injury: borderline mother. The way she shook the stapled chapters of *Understanding the Borderline Mother* I brought home from the hospital in my face, screaming, "Oh, so it's *my* fault you went crazy and stabbed that…witch? It's *my* fault you turned to the Devil?" The way she ripped each page up, threw the shreds all over the kitchen, then threw herself down on the floor, crying in the midst of the chaos she wrought. Back then I picked up each piece of paper and pushed them down into the garbage myself. By the time she was done crying, there was no mess left.

"Sorry. SCI," I finally concede as I pick up each garment, pull them carefully onto velour hangers, then hang them inside the complex organizational system that is her closet. Each section arranged by color and season and fabric ingredients. Focusing on these details helps me keep my emotions in check, my voice from quivering. "I guess…" I pause, not sure how to phrase what I want to say so that I'd get a straight answer. "I'm just…" I try again, then stop. "Doesn't an SCI require more…maintenance? One appointment three weeks away—"

"Oh, I'm pretty sure that blouse is silk, dear. Don't mix it in with the satins. You'll confuse me."

I close my eyes. Take a breath. *You cannot control anything but yourself.* Pull the ruby blouse back out of the closet, look at its tag. Sure enough, silk.

"Sorry, Mom," I mutter as I place the hanger among the silks, where it belongs.

"Don't worry about it! I thought the same thing. About the appointment, not the silk. I'd never make that kind of rookie mistake," she laughs. "But there's not much the doctor can do now. I've just got to heal, and healing takes time. No need for unnecessary appointments. Anyway, I've got everything I need to do documented. You know me, I always take all kinds of notes when I talk to my doctors."

I can just imagine my next call with Carla. What she'll say when I regurgitate Mom's sorry excuse about unnecessary appointments.

That I'm doing it again. That I never had the stomach to confront Mom about her bullshit. That I believe everyone, and even when I don't, I'm too cowardly to say so.

But, a part of me whispers, I never had proof she was lying about her cancer, or her autoimmune disorder, or the numbness in her arms and feet, or the fainting that no one could explain, or the continuous infections that seemed to pop up whenever she had strange cuts or wounds. Yes, Carla did claim she saw Mom wrapping rubber bands around her ankles before going to the ER once, and there was that time a doctor found fecal matter inside a cut that she thought was made with a shaving razor. But even if she was lying then, this is different. This isn't a medical condition. It's a car accident. And her car isn't here, it's in the shop. She has a neck collar on. She must really be hurt this time. Why else would she insist I come home and take care of her now?

I open her top drawer, a stack of her silky, lacey underwear in my hand, ready to sort by color and material, when I see them. Three pairs of men's underwear. Briefs, it looks like, and brand new, or close to it. I place her underwear down and pick up a navy pair, unfold them and turn to Mom, an eyebrow raised.

"Oh, those," Mom says, giggling like a schoolgirl. "Roger's." The name sounds familiar, but she definitely never told me she was seeing anyone. Which is strange, because Mom has always told me about the men in her life in disturbing, unwanted detail. I know how they met, when they started dating, when they started having sex, how often it was to start, how much it went down according to her various ailments. I know in-depth details of these men's lives and desires. She even asks me for advice sometimes, as though I, a single mother who spends most of her free time with her daughter, have anything of substance to offer on the subject of love and relationships.

"Didn't I tell you about Roger?" she asks, once again making me wonder if she can see inside my head. She must see something on my face that she interprets as jealousy, because she continues, "Now don't be offended! I wasn't supposed to tell anyone about him and me. We just got to talking while he was giving me the Botox, and—"

"Wait, the plastic surgeon? Didn't you say he was married?"

"Well, yes, but he's been ready to leave her. Awful woman. Called him 'disgusting' and 'worthless' and 'shriveled up.' Which is totally untrue, by the way. He still looks real good naked. Works out and tans and everything. You'd absolutely love him. You and your little Katie."

Her lies are once again becoming my lies. This is how I become culpable.

I fold Roger's underwear back up and place it in her drawer, feeling sweat gather in my armpits. The physical way my body reacts to carrying her secrets, the moral weight of them. Heat that starts under my arms and quickly spreads red across my chest and up my neck, into my cheeks. Like my very body is allergic to her. On those occasions she actually noticed, she'd place a damp hand against my forehead, smile, and tell me I was fine, just a teensy bit warm. Then she'd get me to feel her head in return, insist she needed a cold washcloth right away. That, at least four Tylenol, and a glass of water, and once I got them for her, placed the tablets in her one hand and the glass in her other, once I draped the cool cloth against her skin, she'd smile up at me with such gratitude. "My savior," she'd say. I've always felt so close to her in those moments. So needed and necessary and useful.

"Actually, dear, since you asked about him..." As she trails off, the words wind themselves into a silence that, I know, will soon flush my skin. I place my hand against my throat, as if to slow the crimson.

"Yes, Mom?"

"I was wondering if you could do me a favor."

Apparently, Mom and Roger were having "a rough patch" right

before her accident. His wife had a cancer scare, and now he was trying to break it off with Mom. He didn't know what was good for him, he just knew what was easy, and that was to stay with his wife. But after her life-threatening crash, she'd been doing a lot of thinking, and she thought that he might want to know what had happened, that she was okay, and that she forgave him. She couldn't call him herself, that would be desperate. But maybe I could call him pretending to be a nurse, tell him what had happened, say she'd been calling for him in her sleep. That she was getting released from the hospital soon, and I thought he might want to know. In case he wanted to check in on her, see if she was healing all right. This was so, *so* important to her. If I did this one thing, she'd never ask me for anything again.

The old refrain. Does she really think she'll never ask me for anything again when she says it? Has she any of the times she's said it? Or is the question a mere formality to her, like Roger's marriage, like her appearances at court to "support" me, like her questions about what I needed from her once I was released from the hospital as a once again friendless, but newly infamous teen?

"Give me your phone," I finally say, numb.

"You can't call from there!" she screeches. "He'll know it's me."

"I'm not calling from your phone. I need to write down his number so I can call from a payphone. Maybe even the ones at the hospital. Something not traceable to me, anyway."

"Good thinking," she says as she passes me her phone.

∽⃝∼

I find Roger's wife Marian on Facebook easily enough. Mom had looked at her profile enough that her name came up in the search bar as soon as I typed the letter M. In Marian's profile picture she is smiling wide on the deck of what seems to be a cruise ship, her whole body turned in toward Roger, who, it must be said, does look good for his age. They both do. It's obvious Marian has had work done. Her forehead has that same unnatural smoothness, that same slightly strange stretch of her eyebrows, as Mom's does. She's one of those people who play a lot of Farmville, who shares memes that quote scripture in cursive fonts and pastel colors, who encourages others to donate to this or that Christian charity doing work on whatever issue is topical at the time. It's like she has a spreadsheet of them or something.

Poor, clueless, Christian Marian probably doesn't deserve what I'm about to do. But neither did Hope, back when I was fourteen and feeling smothered by my mother, who kept "accidentally" pulling out the phone jack when we talked for hours after school. I was so sure if I sacrificed Hope—the one person I loved by choice instead of obligation—the powers the demons gave me would let me bring her back. I'd have Hope, have everything I ever wanted, and never have to deal with Mom again. I was so sure that all of this was a test, and I was so close to passing. But Hope didn't deserve to be stabbed, just like I didn't deserve the poison my mother mixed with her love and poured down my throat. These days I was less and less convinced that anyone deserved anything. That didn't seem to be the point. Things happened, and people made choices, and whatever happened, happened. In that way, maybe what I believed as a teen wasn't a delusion, but a misunderstanding. A literalizing of what should have been metaphorical. I did need to sacrifice something if I wanted my life to drastically change—but not a person's literal life, represented by their body, their meat. I needed to sacrifice something closer. Something so close, so enmeshed with myself, that the sting of losing it prevented me from ever sliding back into that comfortable chokehold again. My most valuable thing wasn't what I loved most, but what I feared to live without most. The pillar to which I had so mindlessly shackled myself.

I click open a blank message, attach screenshots of the most incriminating texts—the ones where he asks Mom what she's going to do to him when they met up, what he wants to do to her, what underwear she'll be wearing; the ones where she consoles him about the latest insult his ungrateful wife has slung, where she calls him her "king," where they talk about their love, their future together, how she'll remodel his bathroom once she moves in—making sure that Roger's cell phone number is clearly visible in each one. Each time a message can't hold any more pictures I click send, then, when I finish, I turn Mom's phone off and place it face down on the kitchen table. I fill a glass with cold water, grab four Tylenols, and hold the softest washcloth under the stream of the faucet, wringing it out carefully, then folding it into a rectangle like she likes. I bring them all into her room, and as I run through our old routine, Mom smiles up at me, eyes bright.

"My savior."

MS WRONG

CHANTAL V JOHNSON

ON VALERIE'S FORTIETH BIRTHDAY she decided to order something for herself, something that might alleviate her suffering, a loophole to the void. She had worked very hard for many years and had amassed significant wealth. But what should she buy? She decided to consult her friends.

Aviva made a strong pitch for a Progeny Bot. "Look," she said, while buzzing around her kitchen stacking and storing various bowls, stemware, and niche cooking instruments, "I never thought I'd want one of these. You remember how I was back in the day. Buttoned up and corporate during the week, then topless and coked out come Saturday, meeting randoms in hotels. That time you had to come get me in Vegas after the cowboy conman stole all my credit cards? Best sex of my life though, ha ha. Still think about him at night, ha ha. He was an actual genius. My secret life that no one would ever suspect! And you rescued me non-judgmentally. Derek called me a prude the other day and in my head I'm like, tell that to the five members of your favorite indie rock band who gangbanged me *consensually* when I was twenty-two. He would never be able to listen to them again if he knew. Do you think I'm a bad person for like, keeping all that from him?"

"No way," Valerie said. "Can't tell a man everything. The key is to make him think you have. Besides, life is hard and *I Am Not You Are*

Not Me Or Are You? is a great record. Let Derek have that, at least!"

"Anyway, getting *it* reduced those urges considerably. My days have a shape now. Of course, it was a bummer not getting approved to have bio kids. Who knew I'd have a high likelihood of perpetrating physical and emotional neglect?"

Valerie fidgeted with the starfish charm on her necklace, unsure what to say. Then, a little voice: "What's 'neglect'?"

Valerie and Aviva turned to face Polly, who had quietly entered the room. It had been manufactured to look like the biological spawn of Aviva and Derek, possessing Aviva's almond eyes and Derek's slight underbite, Aviva's impishness and Derek's roving intelligence.

"It's when a human isn't taken care of, Polly. But you don't have to worry about that."

"Because you'll always take care of me?"

"No, silly. Because you're not human!"

Everyone laughed.

"I'll show you something cool, Val. What music are you obsessed with right now?"

"Anarchist GynoThrash from like, Sweden."

Aviva opened Polly's back case, revealing a foreign maze of circuitry. She clicked buttons, flipped switches, typed something. A loud, garbled static. "Ugh, so annoying," Aviva said. Then she gave Polly a swift kick in the back. "Now that we've had it for a while it can get a little glitchy. Might be dust caught…I'll just blast it with the compressed air, put this dishrag into its mouth, and reboot."

"I love Salem's Mistress!" Polly said suddenly, spitting out the dishrag and coming online.

"What do you love about them, specifically?" Valerie asked.

"The screaming! A woman's scream is so much better than a man's!" Then it squealed and leapt at Valerie, sticky little fingers encircling her neck. "I love you!"

"I love you too. Now sit on my lap and let me tell you why Malcolm McLaren is evil..."

Valerie left Aviva's feeling like an omnipotent entity, the sole and endless source of wisdom and nourishment. She wasn't sure about that dishrag, though.

∽◎◝

Q felt strongly that Valerie should invest in an Impenetrable Body Mod.

"It sounds cool," Valerie said. "But all three holes? Permanently? I don't know if I could seal my mouth. I have, as they say, the gift of gab!"

Q typed on a mobile keypad currently affixed to her stomach, accordion-style. Then a digital replica of her old voice got piped out from a tiny speaker in her neck: *You get used to it, and honestly, as a writer, this works for me. I find that I have better control of my cadences now. I am learning, for instance, how to think iambically. "And the highest levels of prosody / reveal themselves sometimes to me..."*

"Now I love a good rhythm, but I worry I might get lonely in there, all closed up like unhusked corn."

I am less lonely now than I have ever been, Q said. *I exist in community with other impenetrables, who have organized into a micro-society based on an ethics of mutual care. The sex? Oh, Valerie, deprogram thyself. The holeless are fucking in all kinds of new ways. Grazing is foreplay, and rubbing can be sex! Just last week I came from a gently affirming arm squeeze. And all my paranoia about being attacked from behind, from the side, from below? Completely gone.*

Valerie felt a rush. "Having no fear sounds nice."

Also, because of that big class action, there's a mandatory trial period. As long as you cancel within the seven-day window the sheath won't seal permanently.

Valerie chose a matte black sheath with the optional neck armor upgrade. She didn't want to be raped *or* strangled. The sheath had been custom-made to fit her body exactly. She'd never been good at identifying materials, but she guessed that it was something between leather and...steel? She didn't slip it on so much as she entered it, and as she did, the suit seemed to respond, its super-strong fibers slowly closing up around her. It felt kind of sexy, having a second skin. Being encased. She enjoyed the feeling of the metal on her pubic bone and appreciated the silicone-lined labial strip. Protection *and* comfort! A woman definitely designed this.

Initially, Valerie felt safer in public. For the first time in her life, she explored the city at night, fearing neither empty alley nor dark corner. A great sense of power came over her. I can daydream and zone out! I can ignore whoever I want! I can be mean...indiscriminately! But around night four she had a thought: if the sheath created new ways of fucking, didn't that necessarily mean that it created new ways to get fucked? If touching was sex, what was a graze unwanted?

The crush of the urban crowd felt newly dangerous. Valerie's horrible thoughts, lurid thoughts, ruining everything, all of the time! On day seven, minutes before the sheath was set to seal, she found herself trapped on a bus at rush hour. The inescapable flesh of unsheathed strangers began to have an air of atrocity. So the body now was modified, but not the mind, she realized, no sheath for the mind. In a panic, she forced herself through the dense mass, then got popped out onto a potholed road. She crouched down on the curb, undid a tiny zipper near her right ankle, and pushed the cancellation button, which was supposed to start the shedding process. Nothing happened.

Get it off me! Valerie type-screamed while jamming the button. It was then that she noticed another impenetrable, tall and lithe, confidently gliding down the sidewalk with an array of shopping bags.

Valerie waved her over. *HELP ME GET THIS OFF!* The stranger expertly dug up into her leg, reached the button, held it. The sheath hissed and began to slowly unzip itself. *Have to hold it down for five seconds,* she said. Then she gathered her bags and was off, leaving Valerie alone and naked, except for her starfish necklace.

Rapeable again, Valerie thought, immediately and undeniably rapeable. But in the ways she knew, the familiar ways.

∾℘∾

The following months were difficult, as Valerie struggled to recover from the sheath debacle. So far it seemed that the void-fillers were only deepening the void. Would she interrogate that possibility at all, would she see it through to its logical end? Fat chance.

One night when her arousal returned, Valerie went to her favorite bar, Petra's, to look for prospects. She was very much "on the prowl." This was a dumb idea, as it was impossible to start any intrigue in person these days, but the music was good: German ambient jazz that made her feel alluring and unholy. She sat at the intimate, crescent-shaped bar admiring the drink-maker. He kept his hair long, like the ideal man should. She couldn't help but flirt with him, the way she flirted with men, which was to treat them as if they were women in the 1970s and she was a man who could say whatever she wanted to them. After encouraging him to keep his hair long and petting him a little, she ordered a Tom Collins, which he made way over there. "I don't experience rejection sensitivity, you know!" she called out to him. Then, to herself: not sensitive to that. He wanted her in the other universe, *that's* for sure. Worshipped her there.

Valerie's immediate options were limited to a couple of heavy-drinking males: one lean (under thirty) and one pudgy (decidedly over). Pudgy Man was reading a big book by a Croatian author. The polyphonic novel was back, baby! He kept glancing over, and Valerie thought that if he were hotter she would really have to look that title up online. He did cross his legs though, and she sensed he did this to titillate her, as if he knew her thoughts on the matter: the ideal man crosses his legs.

The second one was so young and cute that he didn't need to affect a literary air; phone-as-prop sufficed for him! He was sitting close enough that, by sneaking peripheral glances, Valerie was able to spy him watching the personal videos of various women. He did this in a listless and drugged way. Valerie wiggled around a little, sending out a sex flare, but the Low-Value Lean Boy didn't register her at all. Waiting for one of those mousy white women to step out of the screen, probably. She of messy bun and lukewarm opinion. *Does that make sense? I'm fine with whatever. Or we could go there.*

A woman sat in the empty stool next to Valerie. She sounded older, but what if she was more attractive? Valerie stiffened, felt herself getting angry. But before her competitive spirit could get going, the woman ordered a Batanga. "Do you know what that is?" she added, in a half-flirty, half-patronizing way that made Valerie smirk. Who was this chick?

Jackie Price was a technician over at Aphrodite Labs. They got to talking and drinking, and Jackie let slip that she had grown up in Little Rock. "Oh no," Valerie said. "I don't trust anyone from Arkansas. A man from Arkansas threw me in a river once. I couldn't swim! I've chosen to take that out on the entire state."

"Well don't count me as one of them," Jackie said. "I hitchhiked out of there the day I learned I was pregnant."

Valerie asked how long ago that was.

"Oh, thirty-five years or so. If there'd been a show called *13 and Pregnant* back then I might have kept that baby."

Valerie laughed and relaxed a little.

"Let me see that charm you keep fiddling with," Jackie said.

Valerie held out her necklace. "Pretty cool, huh? I love starfish because they regenerate—just like me!" She said this last bit in a little girl voice. Now it was Jackie's turn to relax.

Valerie went back to openly ogling the bartender. "He's *so hairy.* Chest hair bursting out of that shirt. I wonder what's going on with the nipples. Can you imagine what he would look like in this skirt, the skirt that I am wearing? Look at those legs!"

The man went on ignoring Valerie's efforts, and Jackie grinned. "You know," she said, "because of my work at the lab, I'm able to procure certain quantities of human pheromone. You might try it on your long-limbed fellow over there."

Valerie had heard of these women who go around drugging men for radical sex. She'd thought it was just an urban legend, like the chupacabra or enduring contentment.

Jackie pulled out one of those old-timey crystal perfume bottles, the kind with a balloon pump and a tassel at the end. "What I like to do is tell them I have a perfume I want them to smell. I don't do this flirtatiously, but as a kind of trivia. 'Can you tell me what this smells like?' Men love to demonstrate esoteric knowledge. When your hairy guy leans in, he'll be expecting you to spray the air in front of him, but you get in there and spray him up the nose. Let him try to ignore you after that!"

Jackie said she didn't want to have to do this to men. "I'd love to strike something up naturally, but that's nearly impossible now."

The woman from Little Rock had a point. These days most guys were digitals. As to the rest, they could only get off in highly specific ways you could never predict, so that you'd be on a date wondering: must he throttle me, or *wear* me? If I am to be worn by him, can that happen alone, or does it have to be in a group setting? Interrogating these practices was out of the question, too, because of a little concept called freedom. People are sly. They know how to make their compulsions look like the thing they want.

"What about the ethical angle here?" Valerie asked. "The consent angle."

Jackie explained that the spray only "worked" if a prospect had some attraction to you to begin with. "It's like how gene expression can be encouraged by the environment. The spray is like, an environmental nudge."

Valerie pondered this. Nudging someone seemed way less problematic than drugging them. "So if some part of him wants me, the spray will like, activate that part of him?"

"Exactly! It just takes the effort out of it for you. Also—and this is key—it sexually deprograms them. For a few hours, they are attuned to *you* specifically. They want what you want, even if you can't articulate what that is!"

Valerie had always dreamed of a pure, moment-to-moment sexuality, one untouched by societal norms, technology, or like, a dude's childhood. She watched her man make a perfect martini, dirty and dry. He tucked his hair behind his ear before he poured it.

"I learn best by observing," Valerie said. "So why don't you go first?"

Jackie sidled up to the Lean Boy. "I'm old enough to be your stepmama," she told him. "But something tells me that intrigues you."

ॐ

Sure enough, the mixologist had looked as good in her skirt as he looked out of it. A wonderful time was had by all. But then the pheromones wore off.

"Don't touch me like that," he said suddenly.

"Why can't I?"

"It's like you're pawing at me."

"I'm *admiring* you."

"And then there's how you're looking at me while doing it."

"What's the way?" Valerie asked. "What's the one way you can come?" And then she did that to him.

∽◎∼

Valerie spent the rest of that year going out "spraying" with Jackie. She bagged all kinds of guys, marking types off her checklist, keeping notes of the outfits she put them in. She liked to think that, in addition to becoming a major league slut like Aviva, she was also doing good in the world. Because maybe one day the middleweight boxer she'd accessorized while sprayed would look at a string of pearls with desire when he was sober. And maybe he'd lovingly reach out to touch them. Next thing you know, that big man is wearing pearls in the ring.

Over time though, Valerie grew frustrated at how the spray wore off, and how you could only use it on the same person a few times before they became desensitized to it. Also, while participating in a gender revolution was nice, she couldn't stop thinking about this ideal man of hers.

She broached the subject with Jackie. "My friend has one of those robot kids—can I do that but with like, a guy?"

"Sweetheart, a woman as rich as you can buy anything. You just come on down to the lab next week with a list of your requirements, and we'll see what we can cook up."

∽◎∼

"I have to fill out this questionnaire," she told Q and Aviva. "To discern the qualities and traits I value most in someone. Physically I think I've got a handle on it: long hair, nose like a hawk. He should be into sharing clothes and being regarded, but still able to plow me when I need it. I struggle with the personality side. What I'd like is to never get bored with them, to never want to extinguish their spirit out of contempt. What are *those* qualities? What makes a man *inextinguishable?*"

Q suggested an extremely original guy. *You need someone imaginative, full of surprises. Someone who will always entertain you, especially when your mind goes blank for days on end. Let's pull the plug on Coma Girl once and for all.*

This was an unfortunate childhood sobriquet. "You know what, Q? It's not selective mutism if you have nothing to say."

Aviva said it wasn't just originality, but independence that Valerie needed.

"But male independence scares me!"

"That's because you think an independent man will be violent. But I actually like to be a little afraid of Derek. It keeps me in line. Not in a subservient way, at least, not subservient to him. I'm subservient to *me*, to my own cruelty."

So Valerie went over to Aphrodite Labs and told Jackie: "Hair like a metal drummer and legs that can work a micro-mini. As to personality, I want him to be independent and sui generis! His mind should move very quickly! Quicker than mine! Away from mine! So different from me, so not-me! And I don't want him to feel like a robot, either, so hide that circuitry panel somehow and don't ship him to me. After all I've been through in life, I deserve a meet-cute."

∽◎◯

Jackie set it up so that they'd "meet" at a coffee shop. She said Valerie would be able to identify her Twin Flame robot by its long hair and a "conspicuous tattoo of great personal significance."

As soon as she saw Gregory, she knew. Hair to the mid-back and a face that would've been worshipped by ancient societies, legs that made Valerie all tingly, legs that drove Valerie up the wall! Also, it had a giant starfish tattoo on its right forearm. An hour into their conversation, they were holding hands. A month later, they moved in together.

Gregory had been programmed to be an installation artist with a prior history as a theater actor. This was perfect for Valerie, since many of her sexual fantasies required weeks of advanced planning and elaborately constructed sets. Human males made her feel bad about her proclivities unless she sprayed them, but not Gregory. Her robot man seemed perfectly happy to spend a whole weekend building a craggy ocean set for a carnal mermaid adventure.

Its insights into her were fantastic. "How can I trust anything you say?" she screamed at it once. "Your favorite show is *Sensitive Mobsters*! The therapy scenes don't invalidate the killings, beatings, and rapes, you know! How could you focus on the therapy, when the killings, beatings, and rapes are *right there*?"

Instead of hitting her with its robot hands, Gregory laughed and said she was absurd. "Your past clouds your judgment," it continued, kissing her on the forehead. "Why don't we watch it together while I swaddle you?" An hour later, Valerie was weeping while it rocked her back and forth. How original, she thought. I would literally never think of doing this! Onscreen, a head was being kicked in and children were in danger. Little Valerie sucked her thumb and squeezed her plushie. "I appreciate the jump cuts!" she squealed.

They went on like this for years, until The Big Fight. One day Valerie was squatting in the middle of the forest floor they'd constructed to act out her cryptozoology fantasy (Gregory was a creature made of moss and she its special human friend—she'd keep its existence a secret, under *one condition*). They had processed the experience and were looking for her leathers.

"Let's just go," Gregory said. "We're late for the concert, and you can get a new bodysuit later."

"I don't want a new bodysuit! I want *my* bodysuit, the one I spent thousands of dollars on, the one that was custom-made for me, the one I look the hottest in!"

They worked through it on a surface level, but the argument had made a crack. Resentment flowed through it first, then contempt. Gregory hadn't lived a human life, didn't know what it was like to be treated like a dog *as a human*. Couldn't conceive of how hard Valerie had worked to acquire not only wealth but also the rudimentary emotional and social skills necessary to be a functioning member of society. Gregory's entire past was an idyllic concoction of still-together parents from the professional class and adoring siblings who never quarreled, a synthetic backstory contrived only to provide the robot with the secure attachment that Valerie had requested. Gregory's previously desirable traits—optimism, curiosity, good humor, and spontaneity—began, over time, to seem hollow, naïve, and unearned, mere byproducts of a not-human nature. Valerie started fantasizing about ripping open its back panel and dumping boiling water on it. Or of setting it on fire and pushing it down the stairs. A hammer to the face maybe. What an experientially privileged fuck! Robot loving was not for her, it was clear. She packed quickly, left a note: *Couldn't hack it. To decommission yourself, head to Aphrodite Labs.*

∽☙∼

Valerie lived abroad awhile before returning to her home country, and to Petra's. "Thought I might find you here," she said to a sixty-something Jackie, chatting up a too-young man in nurse's scrubs.

"I just want to say I'm sorry about what Aphrodite did to you back then, and for my role in it. I tried to tell you in person, but it seems you went off to see the world."

"Why are you apologizing? It's my fault Gregory and I didn't work out."

"Who's Gregory?"

"That's what they named my Twin Flame. It was great for a while but I just couldn't do it long-term. Too set in my ways to cross the species divide, it seems."

"Listen, Val, Aphrodite never sent you a Twin Flame."

"Of course they did! The day of the meet, I went to the café just like you said. I met someone with long hair, a starfish tattoo, and pretty much all the qualities I requested in that questionnaire. We 'fell in love' and lived together for several years."

"I'm telling you, Val. You were a mark. You were…my mark. Aphrodite found out I was stealing pheromone and they threatened to fire me. I knew they were in financial trouble, and since you were rich and all, I—well, I promised them your money. The truth is that Aphrodite could only do kid robots. They didn't have the technology to program normal adult human responses, let alone all the hyper-specific and wacky stuff you wanted. Everything I told you about the project was a lie, even the questionnaire. I took those questions from old *Glamour*s, online astrology scammers, and low-validity personality tests."

"But Gregory was like—something out of a fantasy! It sat on my lap wearing fifteenth-century milkmaid's apparel, telling me and only me all of its milkmaid secrets!"

"Well, it sounds like he really loved you, honey. And the age-old art of performance. Also: role reversal."

Valerie sipped her drink and pouted.

"It seems you have a choice to make, Val. You can go in search of the man who just may be your Mr. Right, humble yourself before him, and, should he forgive you, set off down the long, winding, difficult road of true intimacy and vulnerability, or…"

"What's behind Door Number Two?"

Jackie took out a small glass spray bottle, delicate and bejeweled. Then she pointed to the young man next to her and winked.

HOLES

ALICE ASH

THE DAUGHTER IS TOO young to work, but the mother is a perfect waitress. She has a wide smile, light brown skin; they call her *golden*. She has a pale swirl of hair on top of her head and a slight figure, hands like two dancing birds.

The mother can work as a waitress, serving people canapés, hovering inconspicuously behind a tray of fussy little cakes and jellies with red insides: sticky hearts. The daughter has heard the mother; she speaks: "ohs," "ums," and "ahs"—she often says "*of course.*"

"of course"

"of course"

"of course"

It's hard, *so hard*, to afford a babysitter, but the daughter is only a young girl and she won't cause any trouble, she'll just sit still; the girl will wait for her mother to finish waitressing. She is hiding out in Pansy Berry's kitchen, listening to the twittering, the powerful bursts of laughter that peal through the quilted wallpaper and burrow through the giant gilded frames containing portraits of the ancestral bless-ed, their painted bodies definite, covered all over with velvet, little medals, animal skins.

It seems like there is little separating the daughter from the bub-

bling chatter of the party, the laughter and the music. There is just
the wall, the paper, the portrait, and a small, hollow space inside
the plaster. The space is scattered with dust and rubble—over three
hundred different insects. There is a mouse. She has dragged herself
back into the wall, full of poison and bad cheese. The mouse holds a
crumb of yellow for her babies, still hidden inside their nest of paper
and feces. That rich, lofty laughter has red claws, it scratches its way
through all this and finds the daughter where she is sitting, licking
spoons in Pansy's kitchen, fidgeting inside her best clothes.

Pansy will pluck the daughter from the kitchen later; she will be
paraded around, A Little Helper, because she is pretty—thinned by
her father, who had been so fair that he had faded away, a ghost, a
sliver of useless soap in a bathtub—and the people at the party will
want to see the pretty child.

At home, the daughter has a compact mirror with a tab that
snaps when you press it; the daughter likes things like this very much,
things that open and close. Pansy is wearing a locket on a purple
ribbon, and this locket enthralls the daughter. The daughter keeps
forgetting about her little tray of éclairs and custard tarts, becoming
annoyed—*won't you just let me see*—and Pansy is laughing, looking
pointedly at the mother, although the mother doesn't see her because
she is still delivering champagne and special cocktails to the guests.
The mother has to serve the guests, slumped on sofas and against
pianos, those who are dancing and have their faces scrunched up, as
though they are in tremendous pain.

The daughter is tired and wearing too-small shoes that are cruel
at the toe, and a man in a purple suit grabs her as she passes with
her tray. "Pretty girls don't scowl," he says, shaking her a little bit,
and then he goes back to his conversation. The man is eating while
he talks; he chews a custard tart with his mouth open and threads of
custard-saliva join his canine teeth, like violin strings. The daughter

looks at the mother amongst the colorful bodies of the guests; she is grinning inanely, her eyes glossy, her trays glinting, one in each hand. Perhaps the daughter will take the trays, smash them together until everyone is watching, then she will screech and scowl, tear at the purple shirt and use the dainty little cake knife to draw brilliant curves—semicircles—across the man's chest: smiles! But the daughter doesn't do any of this; would the daughter ever do something so completely awful? The daughter behaves herself, as she always does.

When it is truly late, the mother asks Pansy about night buses, and Pansy's cheeks and forehead speckle pink; she says that she has *no idea* about night buses. The mother should have arranged transport *before* the party. Pansy is laughing loudly with her guests while the daughter pulls on her sleeve, and finally she drags the daughter over to a corner to open the locket. There is a small picture there. The daughter looks at the picture and then at Pansy's face.

"That's you," she says.

It is a portrait of Pansy as a young woman, cascades of brown hair filling the frame and a black beauty spot on top of her greasy pink lips, smiling wide, like fishskin. *Pretty girls don't scowl.* The daughter looks at the real Pansy Berry, standing in front of her—she is probably the same age as the mother, but she is beautiful, her head perched atop the flurries of her pink satin dress and the green ostrich feathers, little beads of diamonds all around her throat; and the golden wallpaper glows behind her head.

"When I was young," Pansy says, breathing deeply. And then she packs the mother and the daughter out of the house, just as she will later pack away the waiters; the half-eaten pork roast; the broken champagne flutes; and the crocodile skin handbag that was left, mysteriously, inside one of the flowerpots.

∽⊘〜

The daughter is still wearing her party dress when she takes off her smile and places it carefully in the big hole that she has dug at the bottom of the garden. Nobody knows about the hole, but she looks down into it and feels satisfied when she sees her smile safely stowed down there. It is just her smile; there are no teeth between her empty lips, just black dirt and worms. The daughter takes a match and burns the space beside her philtrum. The mark scabs and oozes a little, but now the daughter has a beauty spot, just like Pansy Berry.

∽◎∾

The mother has hurt her knee, so she can no longer run around serving canapés. Nobody wants a hobbling waitress, and Pansy Berry has called the mother to say that there would be no more parties.

But the mother's work shoes remain at Pansy's house—painful patent heels—and Pansy says that she will have them sent on. When the parcel arrives—brown paper and a swirling inky address—it is a different pair of shoes, three sizes too small, and there is a note addressed "Dear Christine." Christine is *obviously* not the mother's name—does Pansy even remember who the mother is? It has only been a week or so since the mother hurt her knee and she worked for Pansy for more than seven years. The daughter imagines Pansy sat quietly between parties, cooing over her locket, the special portrait of her face. The daughter can't decide whether she is angry with the mother or with Pansy Berry—shouldn't her mother be stronger? Shouldn't Pansy Berry care? Pansy would care about the daughter. Hadn't Pansy said that the daughter was a pretty little girl?

The mother doesn't say how she hurt her knee, but the daughter knows. She won't say. The daughter is quiet, but she already sees that the body gets tired;

gets tired;

gets tired;

gets tired.

Now the mother can't serve at the parties, but she is still allowed
to stack shelves at the supermarket, leaning down on her painful
knee.

The daughter visits the mother on her way back from school.
Something tells her, go on, go; look in on your mother. The daughter
sees the mother, down on the floor, pushing packets of rice into the
black space on the shelf. When the mother sees the daughter, she tries
to stand up without her face closing in, a piece of fruit drying out on
a windowsill.

There is a group of foreign exchange students in front of the
daughter, between where her mother is trying to stand and where the
daughter is, closer to the tills. The students are all talking loudly in a
different language; the daughter thinks the language is French. Three
of the students have mobile phones, each receiving texts or calls and
making noises. A large portion of the group is wearing trainers because they are about to go outside and take a long walk around the
city. These trainers are making squeaking sounds on the tile floor.
Above all this noise, the French words, the squeaking of the trainers,
the electronic disturbance from the phones, the daughter still hears
her mother's sharp intake of breath.

∽◦✑

The daughter undoes her leg at the hip. She puts it into the hole,
throws it with real force this time, because she is angry—how could
Pansy Berry just discard her mother like that? Why did the mother
let herself get hurt? She should have made Pansy like her, been different in some way. The daughter's leg still pokes up and out of the

hole; the hole is not deep enough, and the leg just rests there. The daughter feels better though, once her leg is gone, and she can go back to the house, the sagging windows and the gritty pebbledashed walls. *This is the daughter's leg, her leg; her legs don't belong to anybody else.* The daughter sees the mother, limping; she is going up the stairs, the daughter can see her through the little circular window on the stairwell, and she stops to wave before she drags herself inside.

⌀

The daughter doesn't want to be like her mother, packing shelves and getting home so late in the evening, her eyes still blinking to adjust after the endless brightness of the supermarket.

So, the daughter gets a job in a fancy shop. It is a boutique shop—Énigme. The daughter is only thirteen. Too young. Illegal. But when the manager sees her she says, "Such a figure," and sends her into the backroom with a woman named Dancey.

Dancey helps the daughter, gets her changed into the boutique clothing that will be her uniform. There are piles and piles of boutique clothing everywhere, ostrich feathers that are bright, unnatural colors, like green and orange; glass jewels attached with ribbons, like pendulous jellyfish stings; stiff bodices, seizing inside with insect pincers made from animal bones. In the stock room there are fusty little drawers containing seething gems and more feathers that spring out. The daughter still likes things that open and close, and she peeks inside while Dancey is in the toilet. She listens to Dancey retching and sees a drawer full of doll parts, smooth limbs folded over each other; there are no heads or hair. Small, flickering moths crawl around the edges of each drawer, and when the daughter puts her finger in, they all flutter toward it, landing on the surface of her skin.

The boutique clothing hangs off the daughter and the space

where her breasts are supposed to go is empty. The daughter is only *thirteen*. Still, the manager looks at her and claps her hands; she pretends that the daughter is not thirteen; she tells her customers that the daughter is a fully grown woman, one who has a strict diet plan. She does not eat solid food, only soup and water. *So chic*, they whisper.

So chic;

So chic;

So chic.

Women come in and nod at the daughter's flat chest, they want to see her dressed in different outfits, as though she is a mannequin, not a sales assistant.

"Animal print is in this season," the daughter tries, but the manager holds up one finger, telling her to be quiet while the women circle her, looking at the parts of her body that aren't there; *the space in between*. They ask the manager what the daughter is wearing and the manager tells them, smiling. The women all pick up items and take them to the cash desk.

At lunch, Dancey helps the daughter choose a salad and then they sit in the darkness downstairs and eat silently. Dancey keeps looking at the daughter and pushing the leaves around in the little plastic box. The daughter remembers when she used to make spells in the garden while her mother was out working. She would fill a pan with leaves and flowers, and cut her fingertips, holding the blood inside the muddy potion: a brilliant small pain.

∽◎∽

The daughter has been working at Énigme for more than two years, and she pays the mother rent, slipping gold pound coins and crumpled notes into the mother's jacket pockets. The mother's leg is worse now and she wears a brace when she's at home. The brace is bright white, then dirty cream, and it makes her darker leg look like sausage at the top. Despite her hobbling, the mother has planted vegetables on the rumbling patch of grass where the daughter's parts are buried, digging up knobbly carrots and twisted pink radishes for dinner, slathering them with Stork margarine from the tub. And even the withered old apple tree starts to drop ruddy apples onto the grass.

The daughter feels clever, like she has cheated some blade of fate, just like Pansy Berry did. Now the daughter is like Pansy, and soon she'll have enough money saved to buy some of the boutique clothing and maybe then she'll have her own parties, people to serve her, a locket where she can covet her own beauty. The daughter has done everything correctly, and when she gets that pinching feeling, simmering redness that comes when she sees her mother hobbling, she just goes to the bottom of the garden and sits in the cool darkness. If only the mother had been more like the daughter, if only she had an eye for fashion, a way of dressing and of styling her hair. She should have protected herself. Done things differently. Everyone has that opportunity in life.

Now the daughter thinks that she has complete control.

But one day the daughter answers the back door at Énigme, and she sees a grey woman and two children, two little girls. The grey woman has sparkly fabric slung over her shoulders and arms, yet her body and her face and hair is grey. The children are wearing large stained T-shirts and strappy canvas shoes, and the fabric is draped over their heads. It is cold outside. The grey woman looks at the daughter, as though she is trying to recognize her, and then she says, "Dancey?"

"No…" the daughter starts, but now the grey woman is trying to yell past her, into the dark nest of the backroom. The inside of her mouth is pink and wound-like against the surrounding grey.

"Dancey, Dancey," she calls, "I have something that you'll like."

The children are making sounds of discomfort, wheedling, their voices like honey trickling down the back of the daughter's neck, sticky and uncomfortable, full of sweetness and need. The daughter wants to slam the door shut; she feels disgust, her skin crawling. There is something here that the daughter doesn't want to see.

"Dancey has a day off," she lies.

The grey woman's face changes, and she grabs hold of the daughter's arm. "You can buy," she says, and she holds up a dress. The daughter recognizes this dress. It is sewn with individual sequins around the hemline, like a froth of sea. This dress is of extraordinary quality and craftsmanship, hand sewn by Italian merchants who select the finest materials; the dress sells for £2,000 in Énigme. The daughter is confused; she snatches her arm away. The daughter has afforded a silk shirt, using her wages and the Énigme discount she is entitled to.

"I can't…" the daughter is saying, "I don't have the authority…" She sounds weak, she is wheedling now; the daughter glimpses the grey woman's stomach, where the dress had been draped; it looks like a tiny elephant carcass, the skin painted onto curving bones. The daughter tells the grey woman that she should come back to see the manager; she is panicked, feels her new world being trampled, apples plopping to the earth, shriveled and full of maggots, the space in front of her whirling and grey. The daughter is wearing a mask; she is hidden inside her silk shirt. The daughter needs for the shop to be real, for her new life to stay safe inside of Énigme.

"But for you," the grey woman is saying, "for you, only £10."

Colors are flying through the air as the grey woman tries to showcase the dresses, and her grey ribcage heaves and trembles: brittle, bruised. The girls stand on their tiptoes to support the fabric, to pull out its wings and show the belly, the feathers: the skin. These idiots! This idiot woman should charge more! They could build up their lives; there are opportunities everywhere! The daughter feels childish tears at the edges of her eyes. Dresses are sliding from the grey woman's arms and she is screaming at her children to pick them up: "The floor is dirty!"

The daughter starts to edge the door closed. One of the children, the younger girl, has started to cry. It is a soft sound, as though she does not care if anyone hears or not, but still, the sound gets under the daughter's skin, into her ears: the honey.

The music is playing upstairs, the gentle swell of chatter; the daughter can hear the manager's voice rising at the tail end of a compliment. Énigme is a little microclimate: they sell bottles of perfume and the manager spritzes it through the air every morning. They keep the temperature exact, the light shaded by tempered glass, and the women move around inside, protected by the windows and the doors; they are all performing.

The daughter wants to go upstairs; she wants to fold scarves and touch her finger to a fine grain of dust, *My god, it's filthy*, to compliment old, rounded women, gently saying kind things about their coloring, their elegant wrists, their beautiful taste, all in exchange for a touch of their credit cards.

The children are trying to hold onto the slippery material, it tumbles through their hands as though it is alive.

The grey woman is taking deep, wracking breaths. "Please, please," she says, as the door creaks closed, but above all of this, the daughter can hear the grey woman, anger sharpening her voice into a point as she stabs, "Posh bitch."

∽

The mother is planting something by her new herb garden, but before the daughter can reach the tangles of thyme and sharp points of chives, she gestures to her. "Go back to the house," she says. "Apple pie for pudding."

The daughter nods and thanks her mother, who has collected the apples, spent money on real clotted cream at the supermarket; but she isn't even sure she should eat the pie: *What if the manager wants her to model the new kimonos?* And then the daughter feels guilty, thinking about the grey woman and her daughters—when was the last time they had apple pie? A fox is screeching somewhere near the garden and the daughter feels the cold breeze tiptoeing across her neck, but she can't stop picturing the sticky faces of the little girls. The bubbling, pinching feeling begins inside the daughter; she tries to calm herself and breathes very carefully, in through her nose and out through her mouth. Before the daughter goes, she drops her torso into the hole, pushes the earth hurriedly over the top. The mother hums a tune that the daughter remembers from childhood, and the sheen of the daughter's ribs stick through the earth, like a felled animal carcass, and moonlight catches the bones, poking through. A necklace of ants tremble lightly over the surface of the skin.

∽◉∼

The daughter still works at Énigme, still charms the ladies and showcases the grey woman's jewel-encrusted creations. The daughter has to look after herself—she needs the money, wants to better her life. But today the daughter keeps hearing a tapping sound downstairs, in the feathery belly of the shop. There is one day in every year when flying ants come out and zoom around, decimating themselves against shop windows, tangling their crisp bodies into hairstyles, crash-landing into complimentary champagne, their wings spread like a garnish.

This day is today, the flying ant day.

The daughter tries to get on with her jobs, but her hands are shaking and she keeps knocking things, disturbing the mannequins. And then Pansy Berry comes into the shop. It has been ten years, but the daughter grins, says, "Hallo, Pansy." The daughter pulls herself up, to her full height, and then does a strange little curtsey. The daughter is wearing her silk shirt, has her hair styled and her nails painted, an expensive lipstick turning her lips deep, startling pink. Pansy smiles politely and hands the daughter her bag, goes to the other side of the room where she begins to touch the scarves that are hanging from the rack and trembling in the slight breeze. The daughter looks at the back of Pansy's head, her hair still red and lustrous, and listens to her familiar voice. Pansy doesn't even recognize the daughter, the little girl who had handed out custard tarts at her parties.

The daughter realizes that there must've been hundreds of different waitresses serving Pansy's food: the silly little canapés, the tiny fragrant cakes. She watches the window behind Pansy's head, patterned with black bodies, as though a machine is spitting them against the glass. The daughter's heart begins to pound; she wants to grab a handful of the complimentary sherbet lemons that sit by the counter, to stuff them into Pansy's mouth until there is foamy crystal saliva dripping down her chin. Pansy is limping slightly, getting Dancey to run around and hold up dresses for her. She asks for a little chair, and she sits, looking at the dresses. Pansy is wearing toffee-colored heels and she crosses her feet neatly, one over the other.

The daughter cleans, polishing the perfume bottles, glancing at Pansy's face, the smudge of a beauty spot above smeared lips. Pansy is happily chattering away, but her face is frozen in time, and it looks painful, a war of pinpricks and motionless lakes. The daughter sees Dancey trip on the stair, bringing up a bundle of different sizes for Pansy, but Pansy doesn't even notice—she continues chattering away to herself, playing with the jeweled rings on her fingers. When the daughter notices that Pansy is wearing the picture locket, she cannot stop staring; she knows what is inside, behind the gold pattern. The locket hasn't kept Pansy safe after all; even she has become absurd, after all these years. Pansy keeps touching her neck; she tries to talk to the daughter about the flying ants outside—*Would you believe, one of the insects found its way into my car, and I nearly crashed into a woman, her two children were dallying in the road*—but the daughter doesn't hear her, and Pansy starts to go red, to shout at Dancey. She wants Dancey to pick up her belongings, which are scattered around Énigme.

The manager is angry, but the daughter cannot help herself. The ants swoop around like drunken black stars—the manager screams at the daughter to block the gaps around the door, *Where are they coming from!* But the daughter doesn't move. Dancey chases Pansy around the shop, trying to soothe her and still her little toffee heels, to get her back onto the chair where she can be complimented and given a glass of pink Prosecco. Another cluster of flying ants have come up the stairs and are tumbling through the air, drowsy from the scent, and now another comes and another.

Pansy is shouting at the daughter, something that seems to be in another language, words that the daughter does not understand. Even though Pansy's face is still, glacial, the shouting makes the golden locket tremble, surrounded by Pansy's ruffled blouse, silk and pearl beads swaddling it from each side. Underneath the blouse, there is creased and oiled skin, all kinds of smudges and marks of age. Pansy Berry wears Énigme perfume; it is gently corroding the skin there, trying to sizzle it away, to reach down to her breastplate. There are implants, two lenses of silicone interrupting the cauliflower ducts inside her breasts, then her lungs and tissue; a large nodule, like a lazy maraschino cherry, lolling in strawberry mousse. The daughter can see all of this, but she doesn't let it distract her, and she probes the locket with her eyes, melting the gold and letting it drip down into the satin of Pansy's bra.

∽⊚∼

The daughter does not want to take her face off and throw it down into the hole. She has only ever had one face, and it has served her well in Énigme, smiling and winking and nodding. But in the nighttime the daughter keeps waking up and seeing Pansy Berry's face, collapsing down her front, over and over, again and again— there's nothing underneath, just a smooth grey nub. The daughter would rather take her beautiful face now, take it off and be done with it; she does not want to have it taken away from her, to wince through tears and makeup, plastic fillers and painful injections, like the frozen hostess, coveting her locket—*open, close, open, close—what's in between these moments? When does one thing stop being another?*

∽⊚∼

After the daughter was fired, she had emptied her locker of salad tubs and deodorant sticks, then opened her hands to look inside and seen that they were empty.

Now it is snowing, and the daughter has a new job. This is the daughter's third job.

The daughter works at The Silver Spoon, and she does extremely long hours to match the wages she had been receiving at Énigme. The daughter has become dependent on that money, especially now that her mother has lost her job. The supermarket has started using robot cashiers instead of people, shining bland faces made of glass.

The daughter only goes out in the evening and night, and she is bothered in the house by little things that she has not seen before.

The mother has been humming almost constantly, limping around and sewing the curtains, mending rips that have come through time. She has started to sew the two lips that open in the middle, so when the daughter tries to throw the curtains open in the morning, for the new day to begin, she cannot.

The daughter goes to the kitchen, where there are no curtains, and she sees that the mother has been washing the windows with something sticky, and that now the windows won't open either. The daughter knows that she is lucky when the front door *does* open, but she notices that there are pieces of newspaper wedged around the frame. Little birds have made a nest at the top of the newspaper, and they sit, beadily watching the daughter, their eyes quite raw in their sockets.

The daughter walks down the path, pretending that she is feeling jaunty, but really there is a stone in her stomach. The daughter is twenty-one, but it's like her life turning inward, folding up and under the earth.

❧

The Silver Spoon is empty when the daughter comes through the saloon doors. This isn't a nice pub, and the air looks ill under the piss-yellow light, the golden pumps shining sallowly onto the polished wood of the bar. When the bar maids are there, they light the space like chandeliers, their hair and eyes sparkling, fingers leaking long, glistening nails—Charleston Murray only hires attractive staff—but there's no one in today. The daughter shuffles behind the bar, into her spot, and takes off her coat to hang on the peg.

The daughter can tell from the atmosphere, the tinny blues music that is playing on the sound system and the coke tap that has been left, dripping on the side of the metal sink, that Charleston is somewhere around, and she finds him slumped, closer than she had thought. Charleston looks as though a combination of strings are holding different parts of his body in place; he is sagging, but the strings stop his face from sliding down onto the floor around his bar stool; his brown leather jacket is puddling around his waist and his arms, melting chocolate. Charleston Murray is old, like Pansy Berry and the mother, but the daughter has seen him and his young girlfriend, tobacco-stained fingers wrapped in her hair, perched like a sultan on the tan leather in his open-top car, his acrid breath surrounding him like a cloud of gold.

The daughter looks carefully—Charleston is so still, but she knows that he sits like this often, a lizard camouflaged on a branch, waiting for one of the bar maids to make a mistake so that he can snap his jaw and berate her. The daughter cleans the pumps, cuts thin slices of lime with her special knife—smiles!—and bats away the small brown flies that want to land on the green; she checks the bottles and goes down to the stock room to get more crisps and tea bags, and then she stands obediently, waiting for a customer and rocking back and forth on the painful heels the uniform dictates, her eyes being pulled over to Charleston every now and then, still slumped on edge of the bar.

It has been nearly an hour when the daughter decides to make herself a drink. *A bitter lemon*, she thinks; this is what she used to drink with the mother, when she was a little girl, trying to seem grown-up and elegant. The daughter hums peacefully, uncapping the little bottle and taking one of the thin-stemmed glasses from the top shelf. She can feel the glass unsticking from where the shelf has been covered with spits of sugar; the glass lifts, as if from her own skin. The daughter can feel the bubbles as they shoot hysterically up the sides of the glass, climbing a skirt, or a leg. She has the cool weight of the glass in her hand, then the bubbles against the inside of her cheek, and the sugar against her teeth, winding down amongst her nerves:

the fizz

the fizz

the fizz.

But above all of this, right at the centre of this moment, the daughter feels Charleston Murray and his dripping hand, a slab of grizzly meat. He has snuck up behind her, oozing along by the drip trays and the refrigerators, and he is squeezing her buttock and rolling her skin between his fingers.

The little lime knife is serrated and has two points at the end, like the horned pincers of an insect. The daughter expects to feel resistance inside Charleston Murray's other hand, the one lolled on the bar like a tanned snake, but the hand seems to wither, as though it is full of air. Charleston makes no sound as she pushes the knife into the empty sock that is his arm, and then into the very middle of his body, where there must be organs and a spine. The daughter's hand becomes submerged in gooey, sticky mess as Charleston Murray disintegrates, his legs collapsing and then his shoulders folding into the swamp of his lower limbs.

It takes a long time to clear the floor, and later the other girls will find a mess, a sticky patch, perhaps left by a leaking bin bag or one of the pipes gone bad, and they will step over it all evening, pinching their noses and saying, "Ew."

∾

The daughter stands on the edge of the hole. She remembers the mother at Pansy Berry's party, delicately proffering custard tarts and brightly colored macaroons, cocktail sticks that held smiling pickles and globes of pickled onion, the stems of champagne glasses that her mother had handled like the throats of rare orchids. Then the daughter visualizes the lime knife, traveling through the gloop of Charleston Murray. Pansy Berry sitting alone, her locket coming loose as she swills her wine around in the glass. The earth is grey and little balls of yellow apple glow brightly on the surface of the snow; a worm is waving, feasting on the flesh. The daughter steps into her hole. All around her body the roots of plants and trees writhe; there are mice that scuttle back and forth, along the lower wall, insects that bubble and fuss, tides that are almost invisible, but are actually furious armies, waving jagged arms and legs, pincers made to twist and grab.

The daughter lies there, looking up at the white sky until she sees her mother at the edge of the hole. The mother comes with a blanket, lets her good leg flop down into the hole and hums to herself, draping the wool over her daughter. When night falls, the mother and daughter stand. They share the blanket. The two women walk across the garden but they do not go back into the house; their feet leave deep, dark holes in the shimmering snow, and in the streets, the air is full of buzzing and humming.

MANIFESTATION

SARAH ROSE ETTER

Leslie

In a big white bed, men in my mind stabbed me repeatedly with sharp, silver blades. It was the worst and final puncture which woke me in my condo, drenched in fear-sweat, everything bright as heaven: white walls, clear sunlight, the yawning purple mouth of the orchid on the windowsill.

I made a mental note to ask my acupuncturist what the dream meant, as I believed there was a deeper meaning beneath everything that happened to me: things I purchased in the store, people I met at parties, the moment when the highway cleared of traffic just for me. Everything was a sign of abundance.

This is called manifesting. I could manifest anything: a man, a convertible, a sprawling apartment in a secure complex with gates in the front. But there are certain people who cannot manifest. They are simply blocked. They must do the work to unblock their blessings.

I was blocked before I began my personal work in order to become a manifestor. Some days, all of the pain of my life would rise up, a terrifying creature surfacing within the sea of me, so much pain that I could feel it changing my eyes, warping my face. But with the program, I could fight the pain back down with meditations, visualizations, deep breathing: manifestation.

After the dream of the men with the knives, it was a predictable morning: My husband already at work, a deep stretch in the sheets, the strong coffee already prepared on the counter by the invisible hands of my maid, all the bad news in the headlines which I discarded, the dog on the leash, the lavender burst of the sunrise, the workers arriving at the construction site for new condos across the street, red leaves like viscera on the sidewalk, all of that.

I carried a certain set of crystals in my jacket pocket to increase my magnetism so more manifestations would come to me: quartz, selenite, citrine. In that clear sunshine, beneath that clear blue sky, I felt sure I could call anything into my field, anything I wanted could be mine. All I had to do was ask. The proof was everywhere: In my condo, in the diamond on my finger, in the rich peacefulness of the neighborhood.

How many blocks did we walk? Ten, maybe eleven. Past the gourmet convenience store, past the neighbor's pristine lawns, in the sweet quiet of morning, over the swell of the road, and then past that to the field the dog loved. I bent down to unclip her leash, and she sprang across the long stretch of green. I threw her ball a few times, and she brought it back for a treat each time. This was our ritual. This, too, was manifestation.

Anyway, it was after that. After the field. We continued on our loop, and we passed the corner, you know the one with a small bus stop: One bench and a sign, a gesture toward the option to cross town. You could, if you wanted to, board a bus and be taken somewhere else. Hardly anyone here took it, but the option was always there. You only had to make the effort. You only had to get the time just right.

The stop was usually empty, but it wasn't that day. That day, she was there.

A portrait of the woman on the bus stop bench: Choppy, erratic, short, strawberry blonde hair, pale and freckled skin which spilled out of her tank top at the arms and belly, denim shorts, sneakers which were once bright but now faded to a range of pastels. The stained tank top said LIGHT IT UP in scrawled blue text. At her feet, two bloody bandages.

Against the pristine landscape of the neighborhood, she was jarring. Beyond her were immaculate green trees, new buildings, fresh high-rises, everything that she wasn't.

The dog went, tail wagging and tongue out, right up to the woman, as dogs do. The woman petted the dog's head, slowly. For a moment, her hand was connected to the dog which was connected to me by the leash, and like all things in the world, we were briefly interconnected, a web.

"This is a good dog," she said. "She's a good dog, isn't she? I can tell."

"Thank you. Yes, she's pretty good."

"A very good dog."

"Pretty good," I corrected. "She is bad sometimes."

An awkward beat passed.

"Don't I know you?" she asked.

I looked into her face but no memory registered. "No, I don't believe so."

A strange flinch crossed her face, a wince. "You think I'm homeless, don't you?" she asked.

Another beat. Her eyes were a pale blue, so pale as to be almost white, ghostly, two eerie lights, her eyes were the kind of eyes you would never forget if you saw them even once. I felt as though she could see through my skin with those eyes, piercing, down into the soft mysterious shapes of the organs inside of me.

"No," I said. "You're just a person waiting for the bus."

"Well, you know, I just missed the bus."

"That's the worst."

"A lot of things are the worst."

"That's true."

"Is your dog truly good?"

"What do you mean?"

"Well, some dogs are truly good and some are truly bad."

I balanced the trueness of good and bad in my mind. How much had the dog given and how much had the dog taken away? Could you calculate it that way? I always thought evil hung in the sky above our heads, the black whorl of it, a portal to darkness. That's where storms came from—when the evil got too great and God had to release some of it down on us. We had to pay a little bit for it.

"She's truly good," I said. "I consider her to be truly good, now that I think of it."

"I'm sure you are on your way somewhere."

I wasn't. I was just walking the dog. But I nodded anyway. That's lying.

"Everyone is on their way somewhere," I said. "You are too."

"That's right, I guess. I'm on my way somewhere. I know you're on your way somewhere too. You look like you are on your way somewhere," she repeated.

The sentence folded back in on itself, it was almost a glitch.

"But I wondered if you could help me?" she asked.

I tilted my head. "How?"

"I missed the bus," she said. "And the next one doesn't come for two hours."

The buses were spaced out this way, erratically timed.

She scratched her head a little, her strange eyes flicking away, down, maybe in shame.

"So I just...my phone died," she continued. "They just gave me my clothes back and my phone was on 1% battery."

I tilted my head again.

"I, well, I, I tried to self-harm," she said. "They just let me out."

She jammed her wrists out at me, as if it were a confession, and once I saw the wrists, I couldn't believe I hadn't noticed them immediately. Her wrists were freshly scarred, red and raw, wild with knife marks. I winced because she had tried to do it the right way.

"I just want to go home," she said.

The exhaustion on her was palpable. There was a scent to her, too, blood and something fake fresh above that, hospital soap.

"I just want to go home," she repeated.

She resumed petting the dog. But now, I couldn't stop staring at the inside of her wrists, flashing horribly in the sweet light of the sunrise.

"Where are you going?" I asked.

She said an address. It was a place in a rundown part of town.

"What is it, the place that you're going to?" I asked.

"I just need to see him," she mumbled. "If I see him, it will make sense."

"Who is he?"

"You wouldn't understand," she said. "We're tied to each other."

In the manifestation class, the instructors told us to listen to our body for pings. A ping could tell you which street to walk down on your way to work, or which sweater to buy in a store. A ping helped you make a decision: Yes or no, is it right for you, are you blocked or unblocked?

I listened very closely to my body and the ping came: The man was bad for her and I should stay out of it.

"Please just help me get a car to the house," she repeated. Her eyes impaled me, right through my chest.

Another ping came: She was blocked. She couldn't manifest, she wasn't open to receiving, she was living out patterns over and over again. It was up to her to make a change, like I had. It was up to her to open to the pings.

"I don't think I can help you," I said slowly.

She shook her head and glared down at the sidewalk. The dog licked her hand and I tugged the leash to pull the dog away from her scars.

"People like you never help," she said. "Look at you, in this rich neighborhood, not helping anyone but yourself."

"That's not true," I said. "In fact, I do think I can help you in another way. There is a manifestation class later tonight, and I'd love to bring you with me."

"A manifestation class?"

"You'll see. It will teach you how to be open to the gifts of the world. This program changed my life," I said.

"I need help now, not later tonight," she said. "I don't have time for a goddamn manifestation program."

She was even more blocked than I had realized. She wasn't open to the teaching and gifts of the universe. I pulled the piece of citrine from my pocket and handed it to her.

"I think this crystal will absorb some of the negative feelings you are having," I said. "I don't have any sage on me, but this will help."

"Are you out of your fucking mind?" she asked. "I don't need a crystal either. I need to get to him. It's the only thing I need. Give me money for a cab."

"This is the best way I can help you," I said. "It's the only way I can help you help yourself."

I gathered the dog with a whistle and turned.

"Crazy bitch," I heard her whisper under her breath.

My face flushed. My heart kept pounding as I walked home past the field the dog loved, the swell of the road, the neighbor's pristine

lawns, the gourmet convenience store. Every few steps, I looked over
my shoulder to see if she was following me. The scars were just evidence that she was blocked from all of the blessings of the world. All
she had to do was humble herself. All she had to do was ask.

Jessica

Of course she didn't recognize me, the bitch, not all these years later,
not there at the bus stop, I couldn't believe it was her, with her hair
perfectly highlighted and her body perfectly sculpted with that perfect dog, walking down the sidewalk as if she was floating above the
rest of us, even though it was only me that day, at the bus stop, me
and my new scars, the scars life had made me put on myself, and I
was still reeling from the hours in the clinic, the white walls, the doctors putting more white pills on my tongue, the throbbing pain of
the new scars, then they pushed me back out into the insane bright
light of the world, everything suddenly electric in the fresh sunlight
of a new day, a new day to move through, a new day to push myself
through, and of course after I got out, I walked as far as I could until
I got tired and I saw the bus stop, but of course, in a neighborhood
like this, how often does a bus come? I'd tried to flag down a few
cars, all of them gleaming and brand new, all of them convertibles or
being driven by beautiful people who had teeth so white you could
see them gleaming through the windshield, so there I was waiting
with my stupid bandages on my new scars, and the clothes the hospital gave me from the donation pile, and you know I had to go back
to him, I had to find my way back to him, to the man, every woman
needs a man, that's a fact, and he was my man, he is my man, that's
where I was wanting to go before she walked up, in her tight yoga
clothes, marching around at this strange morning hour, at a time

when normal people are at work, and you know what that means? It means she doesn't have to work, and even worse, she didn't recognize me, not for a second, it didn't even cross her mind, she didn't see me and think Jessica? and remember me, remember my face, remember what she'd done to me all those years ago, all those years ago in college, back when I was in love with him and he was in love with me, back when she couldn't stand something like that, even then, couldn't stand not to have everything, she was a devourer and she devoured him, I saw it, how she started to seduce him, first a hand on his bicep while we were at happy hour with friends, how she suddenly always sat next to him, she thought I couldn't see it, the perfectly manicured hand on his bicep, and my heart crawled up into my throat and I felt like I was chewing glass because some things in this world are inevitable, and a woman like Leslie is inevitable, she will get what she wants, and I had to just watch it all unfold, a Cassandra, me, standing there, watching my own future happen to me, and it took a few more weeks, of course, before he stopped walking me to every class and started missing phone calls, then missing dates, then suddenly it was her in his front seat and I was discarded, I was a woman in a dumpster, I was trash, and everyone saw it, the way she paraded him around, the way he became hers, the way life can invert on itself and force you to lose everything you loved and you have to watch it up close, watch love make his eyes go glassy at the sight of her, their hands intertwined, their bodies always pressed up against each other all over the campus and in the lecture halls, and I found it impossible to concentrate, my heart only red shards of glass in my chest, a constant pain, an awful endless stabbing, then of course it went on: after graduation, their marriage, and my slow slip into a gray world where I realized what I was, which was beneath her, the type of woman who lived with less, never got as much, never got him, their wedding announcement online, then the photographs of them together, the giant ring on her finger, the perfect wedding dress, how thin she'd gotten, the way she was glowing, then the condo they bought, and surely soon the baby, a baby, and me what did I get? I got a desk job and a standard-issue boyfriend, I wore sensible cardigans and shoes with rubber soles, I fostered animals, I tried to believe in love again, don't you think I tried? But I had already had a glimpse into another life, a better life, an elevated life with the man she stole, and it was gone, and she had it all, and there I was, typing up the reports at the desk, going home to the man who could have been any man because he wasn't the first man I loved, the man she stole, and then it happened again, the love started fading from his eyes like a dimming sun, I could feel him slipping away, I could feel the gears of the world rotating, I could feel everything: volcanoes erupting in distant lands, trees growing in the jungle, the bursting forth of rain across the long plains of the west, the very stars above our heads burning their light years away, galaxies collapsing and colliding and devouring each other, and there I was with nothing, nothing at all, except the half of another man who used to love me and that should have been mine gone to her, all of it adds up, even if it wasn't conscious, even if I wasn't thinking of her when I did it, when I got the blade, even if I wasn't thinking of her and her husband it was all there, beneath the skin, humming and raging away, an endless fire that only grew more wild, more unstoppable, and when I saw her today, when I saw her and she didn't recognize me, after my two nights in the hospital, after my two nights of being closely watched and observed and pilled, when she didn't even have a flash of recognition, that's how I knew there was true evil in the world, my father had warned me about that, he said "There is true evil in the world and when you see it, you will know by the hairs standing up on the back of your neck," and the hairs on the back of my neck stood up at the bus stop, but it was a different evil, an evil different from murderers and rapists, an evil that's more subtle than that, an evil that doesn't even know it is evil, an evil that will ruin your life while it smiles, blondly, an evil that will take everything from you then forget your face, an evil that will see all of the suffering of the world on your face, in your eyes, and think itself righteous when it presses a small crystal into your open suffering palm.

BUFFALO

ALISON RUMFITT

HELLO! HELLO! I'M SPEAKING to you, sir, if *sir* you are and I think you are a *sir*. You out in the woods, you out there skulking like a nasty little worm between the trees. You *sir* are a *cunt*. You have ruined my life. Not your greatest crime, of course. Your greatest crime is clearly your rape, mutilation, and murder of three women at least. But in doing that you have also committed the crime of destroying me, destroying my whole way of life, my very existence. Yes, that's why I'm standing out here asking you to face me. Oh it's rather chilly and very dark, and, well, every time I hear a twig crack or a bush shake I jump out of my skin, ironically. But I'm out here anyway asking *you* to face me or else I brand you a coward. Am I not the right kind of woman for you, dear? Am I not of the correct anatomy to get you off, Mister Sicko?

The first I heard about it, see, was when the brick came through my window. I had just been standing there, too, where the brick landed. If it had come in a bare few seconds earlier I would have been thunked on the head by it and gone right down. The glass went everywhere. My Persian rug looked like a mosaic, an art piece of a scattered mirror, perhaps a broken disco ball. I could see a hundred little versions of my face looking down in confusion. I looked up at my shattered window, and through it I could see some hooded figures running away into the midmorning. "Ruffians!" I shouted after them, and I heard them laughing to themselves, and I realised with the drop of my gut that I had just made it all worse, hadn't I? Who do I think I am, calling these people *ruffians*. Not a good example of community cohesion, is it? Well, anyway, I picked up the brick and saw there was a note taped to it. There is, of course, always a note taped to a brick thrown through your window. That's a real fact of life, my dear. I hope you're listening to this, this is important. Important stuff to know and be aware of. The note said *sicko perv murderer rapist tranny cunt*. A list of words, not even a sentence, and yet I could put together well enough its message. I wasn't aware of the dead girl yet, I hadn't, in fact, looked at my morning paper which was at that moment lying nervously on my doormat. It's not the first time I've had a message such as this. It's not the first time I've been called a murderer or a rapist, although all the times before those accusations were in the abstract—there had not been a murder or a rape of which I was being accused, people just assumed, by the nature of my being, that I was a murderer and/or a rapist. I am not a murderer or a rapist. Once, when I was a teenager, I looked through the crack of my sister's door and saw her getting undressed. Later, at university, I kissed a girl who seemed visibly uncomfortable and then stopped. I will admit to both of these things, and would put them firmly under the banner of shameful acts of which I am not proud. You are welcome to hate me for that, but the people who hate me, who spit at me in public, doxx me online and, now, throw bricks through my window, the reasons they hate me have nothing to do with those acts. They hate me simply because of what I wear. Can you believe that, dear murderer? Victimized and demonized just for the way I choose to dress? Dressing oneself is the simplest form of self-expression. Every morning, a person wakes up and puts on clothes which will go on to externalize their internal life throughout that day. I am lucky or perhaps unlucky enough to be a person who chooses to dress themselves in a woman's skin.

You can see the predicament we find ourselves in, sir, given that you are someone who seems to apparently delight in skinning women alive. When I put the brick and its accompanying note down on the table I walked, almost automatically, to my door to pick up my local newspaper which had just been delivered. The newspaper was not the only thing on the doormat: there were more notes, which must have been delivered earlier in the morning. They all said essentially the same thing as the note on the brick. And there, on the front cover of that paper, ink still drying, was the explanation for it all: a woman's body had been found in the woods on the other side of town. She had been raped and skinned, apparently alive. A terrible tragedy. A truly heartbreaking thing to happen to somebody. Women face violence from men everywhere they go. Everywhere we go! I am well-known in this town for my predilections. I moved here because, frankly, it was too dangerous for me to reside in a large city. I kept finding myself being followed home, much like, I think, this poor skinned girl was. I was never foolish enough to think that, by living out here, I might find myself immune to hate or even accepted by my community, but I thought—correctly!—that it may not be so dangerous, and that had been the case up until this point. But that brick, those notes, that skinless bloodied corpse. These things brought with them a herald of a darker time.

The cops came later that day, as I thought they would. I was wearing my finest skin suit. If one is going down then one might as well dress well. They came to my door and there I was, skin on, nice blonde curly wig, pearls around my neck, lipstick on my lips. Mwah Mister Officer!

I have eight skin suits at this point. I was blessed with a large inheritance, thanks to my dear departed despicable Daddy, and so I have spent my life gleefully spending it on whatever I please. Eight skin suits of various shapes and sizes although, don't worry, I am not *one of those* people. I do not have any skin suits which feature skin meant to evoke that of a race other than mine. All my skin suits are various shades of pale. And no, obviously, *clearly* they aren't real skin. Try telling that to members of the public! Real skin holds no interest for me. I am not Buffalo Bill. Perhaps you are, dear. You do seem to be carrying out a similar class of crime. I don't really blame people for seeing the skinned corpse of a young woman, seeing me strutting about town in what looks, for all intents and purposes, like a suit made of a woman's skin, and putting them together. At least its more of a motivation for hate than those who attacked me before there was a corpse.

My skin suits are made from a clever mix of plastic, latex and lycra which gives them the appearance of real human skin. My first suit was rather weak, far too rubbery to be believable. But once you know who to contact you can get the *really* good stuff, which is what I now have: skin suits which have fair hair on the arms and legs, skin suits which have visible pores, blemishes and moles. Some people on the forums want their suits to reflect some version of perfection but oh, not I! I'm a real woman and I want a real woman's body, a real woman's skin but not, obviously, a *real woman's* skin. The ideal skin fits like a glove, is made to your exact body shape but also padded underneath to give you curves you may not have otherwise. If you walk around and find that it is squelching or rubbing against your *real* skin then well you simply have a bad suit, dear. Are you listening to all this? I heard something there. A rustle up amongst the trees… is it you? Are you a tree dweller? Oh, silly me. It's a nightjar up there. I can hear its call now.

The cops took me away, and I could tell that they thought they'd found their (wo)man. I went willingly, which, of course, you should never, ever do. But if I held out I thought that it would only get worse. My house would be burned down, maybe it would be burned down anyway whilst I was at the station. The cops were rough with me when they pushed me into the back of their car. Both men. Both of them had large hands, with palms as tough as leather shoes. At the station they brought me a Styrofoam cup of hot black tea which tasted faintly of urine and I wondered which of them had pissed in it. Oh but they couldn't prove it, they couldn't prove it because it wasn't me; I wasn't even in town on the day the girl died, I had multiple airtight alibis. Checkmate! They made me strip off the suit, laughed at the lingerie I wore over it. They laughed at my quote-unquote real body, how lumpy it is in some places, how skinny in others. Cunts, I tell you. Raw, nasty, mean-spirited cunts. But eventually they let me go. They couldn't even try and pin anything on me, there was no way of doing it at all, so they had to just give up. When I returned to my house, rats had gotten in through the broken window and someone had spraypainted *MURDER HOUSE* on my door.

Two weeks of uneasy existence later and I saw, in my morning paper, the grim and yet inevitable news that you had struck again: another girl was dead, her body dumped in the woods, shorn of skin, cunt ripped open. The DNA evidence had gotten them nowhere, although they had found human skin inside of it. Whose skin? Not mine, I know that. Yours, obviously, whoever you are. I sit here on this log, occasionally sweeping the light of my flashlight across the circumference of my vision. I haven't seen you. Maybe you're not even out there, though I think you are. I think you like it out here, don't you? Do you like the quiet and the loneliness? Where do you find the women? Do they happen to be walking here? Why do you prefer girls? Am I girl enough for you? I'm wearing one of my suits now, of course, under my practical clothes. I have to admit, I can't really step outside without wearing one. Not my finest suit, no, one of the lower ones, although this does have lovely soft underarm hair which I think is a good touch. I'm touching my armpit hair now, actually, with my left hand tucked inside of my shirt. I sniff my fingers afterwards and I swear that they smell like real sweat, too.

They didn't take me in after the second body, but it didn't matter to the rest of the town. I am assumed guilty. I can't leave the house now without being screamed at. I put plywood over all my windows, and added extra locks and bolts to all my doors. And still people stand outside and shout at me. Still they rattle pots and pans in the night, spray *pedo* and *rapist* over my door. Someone keeps drawing chalk outlines of girls' prone forms on the pavement. As if I am not a woman, as if I wasn't a little girl once, as if...

Then, a third dead girl. Three girls, each around the same age. Not from here really, just passing through. Two lived out in the trailer park near the falls, and one was staying in a B&B. They were around the same age, but they had different hair color, different eye color, different hopes and dreams. Every town is a conduit for girls to pass through. I have been a girl just passing through myself, have even, if you can believe it, been a girl subject to harassment, stalking and violence. Never been skinned alive, not yet. I'm sure you think you could do it, don't you, my dear? Or am I not your flavour? Would you balk at trying to unsheathe my penis? I think you would, you little coward.

I know you're out there, in the great dark expanse. I've sat here for long enough. I suppose if you're out there you already know I'm here, so let's go for a walk, shall we? I don't know these woods too well. I'm sure you know them better. Are you an outsider, or have you lived in this town for a long time? I noticed that the women you killed were outsiders, young women passing through, maybe turning tricks to make ends meet, so I have to wonder if that's your motivation...some silly facile moral crusade. Well, if it is, let me tell you:

I've turned tricks myself, I've fucked and fucked and sold dope for buttons and peanuts, so if you think you're some kind of moral bastion you better start running to me pronto, cunt. I've done things you wouldn't believe. I've done things that would make your blood curdle into cheese. I think there's a clearing up here, if I remember right. I think past the clearing there's an old church that nobody goes to anymore. I...

I could hear something then. Was that you? I can see something over there. Past the church. Is it you? I...I don't know what I saw. I don't know what I really saw. It wasn't you, I don't think. It was probably just...did I drink a little more than I planned on drinking? Oh, maybe I did, maybe I did. This old church is just a little spooky and the poor bodies buried here must feel so neglected—there are flowers on the graves but only because they've grown here, unbidden. No one ever comes here to leave flowers now. The church doors rotted open. Are you...in there? I can see in the light of my flashlight beam, rats and voles scampering into the shadows once again, crows up in the eves but no, no *you*, whatever *you* are, whatever *you* look like. When I lived in the city, a man followed me home and threatened to slip his butterfly knife beneath my chin to slice my face clean off. *I want to hold your fucking face in my fist*, he said to me. Not the only man to do that. I must have looked into the faces of ten, fifteen different men, all of them saying similar. If they want my purse, I let them have it—I have twenty more, after all. One man, though, he tore open one of my finest skin suits with his blade, and sliced open the "real," as it were, skin beneath it. I slammed him in the face for that. You can take my bag, harass and rape me, but you *cannot* destroy my skin, *good sir*.

Where are you? I expected you to come for me as soon as I stepped foot in these woods. I know I'm not quite your perfect victim, but I'm an easy, confrontational one. I've called you a cunt and implied that your penis is small. I expected you to be a man, not a coward. But you're still hiding from me, aren't you? Look, *fag*, I want to be able to go to the supermarket without having tins of tuna thrown at my head. That's all I want. Is that really, you think, too much to ask? I want to be able to dress up in Paula Brown's new skin suit and go for a leisurely stroll that doesn't end in death and misery. You are the thing that stands in my way. You're not in the old church, clearly, so where are you? Are you out there? Was that actually you, the thing I saw moving? But I don't understand how it would be or how it could be, even. You see, the thing I saw was...

There, that sound. Gosh, what is that? I can only describe it as the sound of a hundred Sweetie wrappers being rustled by the wind. If that sound indicates your presence, then my dear, something is deeply wrong with you. You're not doing a good job as a serial killer if you wear clothing that makes such a loud, obnoxious sound. You must be wearing a colossal cagoule or something. *Swishswishswish, swishswishswish.* I know where that sound is coming from, so, if it really is you, Mr. Skinner, be aware. We both have what one might term a little *skin thing*. If you fancy yourself a Buffalo Bill then I've got bad news for you, you needn't have gone to all that effort. That film made an impression on me too, you see, it made an impression on lots of us, but we were lucky enough to be in possession of a working moral compass: enjoying a woman's skin shouldn't come at the expense of a woman having skin, my dear, that's why we all started wearing these synthetic suits. It's really just the same, if you know where to get them. You feel just as good as if you were wearing real skin. Just as real. Just as authentic. Just as much a woman as if it came from one directly. So if that's your motivation then I hope you know it was all for nothing, and we don't take kindly that you're giving us skin-suit wearers such a bad name. That sound is getting louder. I can't really place where it's coming from. To my left maybe?

If I keep twirling around like a girl in a show shining my flashlight in every corner, perhaps I'll see you, finally, skulking there in some piece of undergrowth. Perhaps heels were not my best idea. With a note of melancholy I kick both of them off.

I keep stumbling. The air feels close here, close and difficult to navigate and…this skin suit fit like a glove, I swear, but now it feels strange, too tight in some areas and too loose in others. What is this? It's hard to breathe. I don't like this, I don't like this at all, I think I made a mistake coming out here—*fuck*, my skin suit just ripped open, and my clothes with it! Are you there? How? That sound? That noise? The sound is so loud, the rustling, the sound of leather rubbing against leather.

I can see you now, if that really is you. Moving through the trees. Not touching the forest floor. A mass of skin. Oh all those girls…well have my skin suit, see if I care. Is this the way back to the church? Yes, yes, I see it now, my clothes and my synthetic skin being pulled off my body in ribbons by unseen hands. How do you like *that*, cunt? Will you choke on the latex? It's so cold out here, and the earth is damp. I stumble into the church but there are no doors to pull shut against you. I can only hope that you are not of God and thus can't enter this ground, not that I myself am a creature of God of course… I am not even sure what I saw. Skin floating in the air like jellyfish in tropical waters, great masses of it, all tumbling around an unseen gravitational centre. And I felt hands…I swear to God I felt hands. Is that you? Did you not like the skin I gave you? Have you seen me, naked as a babe between the pews?

The rustling again. My skin, the skin that was beneath my other skin, feels strange again, contracting and loosening, throbbing, bubbling. Oh God I wish you'd not make it hurt so much, oh God I wish I could just let you have it, but I can see you there blocking the entrance, and I can feel the great tears across my body flaying me. I look down and I can see it, my hands being degloved, as it were, the moonlight making the flesh underneath glisten. My vision goes red with my own blood. I wish I'd been born with the right skin, I think. If I had, then you wouldn't be able to take it from me. Oh take it, I don't care anymore, just be quick about it and leave a pretty crimson corpse.

COMPOSITION

ALIYA WHITELEY

Necrobiome: the community of organisms—including
bacteria, insects, fungi, nematodes, and scavenging animals—
that feed on and decompose dead matter

I FEEL THEIR PRESENCE as I swing open the old gate, and I know the worst. They have swarmed to the house. They are inside.

I run the length of the driveway. The lawn has grown unkempt and weeds poke through, but the building itself remains the same. The shadows cast by the grand pillars of the façade are deep and long, the autumn sun behind them. We never used the front door, so I swerve around the side of the house, through the long grass, to find the veranda doors wide open. Just as I had left them six months ago. As if I could walk in and pick up the conversation where we left it.

Beyond, in the morning room, he lies. Under the gaze of the stuffed stag's head, and the paintings of the foxhunters with their hounds leading the hunt. On the red velvet chaise longue, where I left him.

They have started their work, but they are taking their time over it. He's too good a meal to rush.

The flies, keen and bright-backed, notice my presence first. They tell me they like the sockets that held his eyes. One should never put faith in eyes; I learned that when I was a child. They are not windows to the soul, but doorways to the flesh, all too willing to admit my friends. I greet them and ask them to stop their buzzing for a little while, just to give me silence. They agree, and there is only my breathing, and the ticking of the tall clock. The bacteria work on, and I will not command them to stop. They are like children. They whisper in delight, no longer held in balance. They play hide and seek in his organs.

Litton is dead: that is the truth. That is the picture before me.

৵ঔ৴

I was his darkness, the thing that made him saddest in the world. He always said it was not my fault, but how could he help but resent me? He hated death, and it was my playground.

My first memory is of his face when he found me behind the stables, manipulating the corpse of a small bird. A wren. Its neck had snapped back, its head loose on its body. It had not been dead for long, but the organisms within it had already started the process of decomposition, and they were making sweet sounds in their tasks. They rejoiced in my presence, too—in being watched by one who could call to them, saying *faster*, *slower* in my mind. They were like an orchestra performing for the conductor. *Fast fast fast*, I told them, and watched them strip the wren to the bone, and then break the bones down to nothing. Their speed was incredible. A process that usually takes months reduced to minutes, just because of my instruction.

"Look!" I said to Litton.

"Come away," he said. "Come away, Deb. It's bad. It's a bad thing."

I knew he was wrong, but could not put it into words. Could he not see the beauty of it? His face was a picture—more than that.

A painting of fear and disgust. He was handsome, even in his early teenage years, but he twisted those fine features into such ugliness, and I cried.

He took my hand and pulled me away, squeezing hard.

✺

I take his hand now. The skin is cold and cracked. Frozen. He has been lying here all night. I squeeze to recreate that moment, that pain. He will no longer school me with his emotions, and I can't hurt him in response.

The fungi in the garden are singing.

It's a wet autumn morning; my shoes are still soaked from the dew. They know I'm here, are rising to meet me, and they're so glad of my presence. They have missed me. They have much to tell me: the meals they have eaten, the spores they have spread. Fungi are talkative. Their cacophony, amplified up through the soil, overwhelms me. They are clamouring for their turn with my brother. They moan that the flies have more than their fair share.

They ask me where I have been, and I tell them *travelling*. They understand that. They have grown through the dark themselves.

I had to go. I had to find out what I was, and whether I was alone in my power. I had to discover the limits of it, and this I now know: I am alone. More so now, in this room, than ever before. I wanted Litton to understand my decision. I came back in the hope that he forgave me.

Too late.

Too late, repeat the tiniest of organisms, *too late, too late*, gleeful in his collapsing organs.

I take the biggest throw rug, the one our mother crocheted, from the armchair by the fireplace. She made it from pieces of our old pullovers, unraveled, as we outgrew them. I wrap him in it, tight, snug, then gather the corners and use all my strength to drag him over the polished floorboards, out to the garden. I don't get far. He's so heavy. Down the slope, a little way over the lawn, toward the ornamental fountain. I can't drag him farther, and I don't need to. The clumped voracious strands of the fungi are already underneath us.

I am at the center of a network that would dwarf any great city; I am the general of the greatest army in the world. I unwrap Litton from the throw rug like a present and tell the fungi they can begin. *But leave the skull*, I tell them.

I coax them to be fast and they move, encroach, enter and feast at speed. Then the fruiting bodies, the mushrooms, erupt from his chest, his stomach, his groin: fat, vivid jellies and morels in many colours. They will strip him clean, make him their own. But I will keep his skull as a reminder.

∞℘∽

It was the day that I realised my parents didn't own this fine house and grounds, but were the servants of a rich man who chose not to live there himself. They were caretakers of his greed, his paintings and fine wines, his guns and games.

I was dressed in a plain pinafore, patched. Litton was very much taller than me; well, it seemed that way, at the time. He would have been eleven years of age. We were standing together at the gate, waiting to open it for the car that we had been told to expect. When it arrived, it was a sleek, magnificent beast of silver, roofless, reflecting the sunlight on its curves. The man driving it, black-haired and stiff-jawed, wore sunglasses. I couldn't tell if he looked at us as he cruised by; he didn't turn his head so much as an inch in our direction.

"He owns it all," Litton said. "The house, the gardens. All his.

But he doesn't own us." He stuck two fingers up after the car as it coasted the bend and moved out of sight, and we closed the gate and ran after it, the gravel crunching under our feet.

When we got to the main door, the man had already got out of the car and was talking to our parents, who stood next to one of the pillars, eyes cast down, shoulders slumped. They were not like my parents at all. Who were these sad, cowed underlings? I did not know them. No—worse than that. I did not like them, and I did not wish to be part of them.

I could not hear what the man was saying to them, but it was a tone of command, of disdain. My father replied, something like, "But we're good workers..." And, later, my mother said, "Please." She said it a few times, then, "Where will we go?" Her fear got into me. I crept closer to the car, Litton behind me. I rested my hand, so lightly, on the chrome bumper.

The man looked over his shoulder at us, and I met his gaze. He had removed his sunglasses, and I thought his eyes kind. I smiled at him.

"Get your kid off my car," he said.

I don't suppose I really understood what was happening when he started walking toward me. Neither of my parents moved to intervene as he reached out. Only Litton stepped forward, put himself in front of me. The man didn't stop moving, shouldered Litton to the side. Litton was still small for his age. I watched him fall, his palms and knees hard to the gravel.

The man was upon me, and I called the flies first.

They came fast, as if they had always been waiting for such an order. The sky was black with them. Then they settled upon him, on his suit, his shoes, his face, his swatting hands, and when he opened his mouth to scream, they took their advantage and swarmed inside.

He dropped to the ground, and I called the fungi. Up through the soil beneath the gravel, pushing the little stones aside, creating mycelial strands far too strong for him to break. They made long and dextrous fingers, pushing into his clothes, his skin.

It all happened very quickly. If only my mother and father hadn't tried to intervene. Why did they move to help him, and not me? My anger encompassed them too, and my friends followed my desires. I was young—is that a defense? Yes, I must forgive myself, just as Litton forgave me. I really believe he did.

༄

"It's not your fault," he said, as he tucked me into bed that night. "It's not your fault."

When I came downstairs the next morning, he had already made toast, and the car was nowhere to be seen. I don't know what Litton did with it. There was nothing left of the man, or of my parents. My friends are efficient.

Litton said to me, while I toyed with my crusts, "You're going to be amazing, you know that? You can help so many people. I'll help you learn how. We'll work hard. You'll stop bad guys."

But wasn't I the bad guy? I spent months expecting to be found out, guilty in my shame and fear. Then the disappearance of the owner was ruled a suicide, driving over a cliffside into the sea perhaps. He had a history of abortive attempts, a lucky break for us. I have a few memories of official letters, correspondence that my brother answered in my parents' names, about the house. Could they stay on as housekeepers indefinitely while the estate was processed? They could, my brother wrote carefully in his best handwriting. As far as I know, the house is still in the limbo of litigation.

༄

The enthusiastic frenzy of the fungi draws to a close. The mushrooms die, turn the ground into slime, and the throw rug is left, a sodden mess, from which his clean white skull peeps.

I take it in my hands. It is not smooth and cold, as I imagined, but rough, textured, and very delicate. I hold it up and examine the sockets. It's impossible not to feel like an actor in some mannered play: *Alas, poor Litton.* But the laughter bubbling up in me dies away and leaves me empty once more.

I thank my friends for their quick work and take the skull back to the morning room. I place it on the chaise longue. Litton is back where he belongs.

"Don't look at me like that," I tell him, and it's so familiar, these words, this place. Our last conversation comes back to me in a rush. Like death, memory cannot be denied.

∞

"Don't look at me like that," I said.

Litton was staring at me, sitting straight on the chaise longue, his arms crossed, his entire body tensed. How uptight he was. It only made me more certain that I'd made the right decision.

"Let me come with you," he said. "Please, Deb. Please. Don't do this alone."

"It's time," I told him. "I can't find out who I am with you along."

"You know who you are!" he said. The fact that he had raised his voice told me how upset he was. He had always been the very model of reason, as if acting that way would lead me to do the same.

I shook my head. "It's not so simple."

"Where will you go?"

"Anywhere. Everywhere. There must be others like me. I'll track them down."

"If I come with you, we can look for them together. We can learn more about this gift you have—"

"It's not a gift."

"Then what is it?" His gaze made me uncomfortable; I looked away, to the mounted head of the stag on the wall, but still he talked. "The insects, the mushrooms, even the bacteria in my body would obey you if you called to them. So, what is it, if it's not a gift? It must mean something, Debra. You have to make it mean something."

"Why? To make sense of what I did? Of the time you've spent trying to keep me hidden? You're so—"

"So what?"

The words escaped me; they couldn't be controlled. "So good! You take all the good, don't you get it? There's no room for me. I can never be as good as you."

"Just... try. Stay here, where it's safe, and try. You owe me that much."

I realized, then, that I would always owe him. It was a debt I would never be able to pay.

"I'm going," I told him. "A month. No longer. I have to find out what I'm capable of."

He stood up. "I already know what you're capable of," he said.

It was the closest he ever got to blaming me, and it hurt more than I had thought possible. I shouldn't have done what I did next, but he pushed me to it. He should have known better.

"I'll come back," I said. "And when I do you will be here waiting for me, do you understand? If you try to follow me, if you so much as set foot on the grass outside, I'll let my friends have you. I'll let them take their time."

And I left.

My search for answers took a little longer than I had intended, but still, only half a year has passed since then. I thought he would be long gone, having called my bluff. Didn't he know me well enough to know I was bluffing? I could never have made good on my threat. It was not even within my power; these organisms do not have memories, in the human sense. They live only in the here and now. I envy them that.

I crouch down and look under the chaise longue. There's the gun he used: one of the smaller ones, taken from the cabinet upstairs. It must have dropped from his hand after he pulled the trigger. I wonder why he chose to end it here, in this room. Perhaps it was because he wanted to finish our argument where it started.

I put the gun down, next to his skull. I have no use for it.

I remember that night, after the first deaths, when he put me to bed and told me, *It's not your fault.* I have never argued with him about that. This power, and my temper: neither are my fault. I did not ask to be born, to be made this way. And I've found no answers out there. I'm no closer to being what my brother would have wanted.

I walk out of the house one last time, and I call to everything within my reach. *Come with me,* I tell them. *Come with me now.* By the time I reach the gate I have a frenzied, thrashing tail of flies stretching back behind me. Their gleeful buzz is deafening. The beetles march in line, and the fungi have ripped up the long grass, overturned it all to make a vivid landscape of mushrooms. They make a pretty picture— a much more fetching composition than those old paintings in the morning room. The house itself is dull and grey in comparison. I wonder how I could have ever thought I'd come back to it.

I lead my friends in the direction of the nearest town. We'll start there. Everyone can pay for what I was born as, and what I have become.

THE MONOLITH

CHAYA BHUVANESWAR

1.

Jane Chun knew this much, knew it fiercely: whatever good opinion William Mangan had of her, the new girl could put it into flames. The girl was a former Fulbright scholar who studied modernist poetry at Trinity College in Dublin. Pretty girl, an appealing pinkish-lightish brown. Girl with a name you can't pronounce, hardly worth pronouncing. Arrogant, as one might expect from the CV, though the girl seemed earnest, in her way, and quite down to earth. A poet getting ready to read her work at a small venue. A modest schoolteacher, readying a lecture she'd been researching carefully. That must be the girl's shtick. Her armor against the punishment that comes, in medical school, for being perceived as arrogant. The problem with such people, Jane thought, is that their earnestness becomes a blundering ignorance of how the world works.

The student was only a girl, age twenty-five, while Jane was a woman of the world, but Jane still felt angry and nervous, about this brown girl. And in turn, Jane had been trying to make the girl nervous, daring to ask, in the hearing of nurses, techs, other med students, "Hey, sorry I can't pronounce your name, you, girl, med student, whatever, hey, do you think you might have dyslexia? Or something. You seem to have a problem writing scripts. You keep getting some details slightly wrong. Like, you reverse the PO and the frequency. All the information's there, fine, but it's off somehow."

What this girl—fine, Re-nuke-a, at least phonetically, reminding Jane of the expression "to nuke"—what this girl obviously didn't know: second-year medical students like her aren't even required to write scripts. There's little that they have to do, in point of fact, but soak up knowledge from attendings like Jane, and above all, defer to that knowledge. The student must acknowledge not having knowledge. But Jane had gotten this girl Renuka tied up in knots, convincing her that because of her typos on scripts, her slowness in answering a question or two about the selection of antibiotics for flesh wounds in cancer patients, and worst of all, her habit of occasionally crying by the bedside, actual tears, something Jane hasn't had to worry about since she can't remember—because of all that, Jane made it clear, this Renuka might not even become a doctor. It was true that Jane could at least stop her from being an internist.

Jane might well be able, by telling William what to write, to make sure something terrible was written about Renuka, in as demeaning and damning a tone as possible, in the critical memo, rotation assessment, that goes from William's desk to Renuka's medical school advising dean, and then in turn is read by every residency program in every hospital that would decide whether to train her. They could all bar Renuka from the gates.

It's a deadly efficient, ancient system of patronage and retaliation; Jane herself knew it from the start, was told as much by her many relatives who'd trained in the US, by doctor boyfriends she dated as an undergrad, even by residents who trained her as a medical student, who generously protected her. Which was why William, Jane's own oncology fellowship preceptor from two years ago and now her faculty mentor, nearly the sole determiner of Jane's fate, was someone whose tastes Jane had memorized, whose needs and wants Jane had taken pains to understand. Whose predilection for off-color jokes about nurses' anatomies and about the "secret affair Jane and I have been having for years, ha ha ha ha" were all important to Jane, all the more important because William must intend the jokes as a personal, enduring connection to Jane, which will be valuable to her because he is her mentor. He takes the risk of making those jokes knowing his department chairs, if they ever came to know of them, would say they're in "poor taste." William wrote her a glowing evaluation, recommended her for every clinical and teaching award, has invited her, more than once, to have meals prepared by his wife, in his home. So, joking with William, not in the way Jane might find enjoyable, but in the way that William wants, is essential for an ambitious young doctor, male or female. Part of career cultivation.

Jane is unusually ambitious. She even blew him once, William the charmer, her mentor, though William has always pretended it never happened. He's fifty-seven years old now, to Jane's (extremely young-looking) thirty-three, but once, just one time, about six years ago, they were taking a flight together to a conference in New York, Jane seated beside him in coach, close enough for plenty of seemingly accidental touch. Their chatting was pleasant until talk petered out. Jane, after consuming three of those small bottles of wine one had to buy for cash in coach, which William hadn't bought for her, wasn't as sleepy as she'd expected to be. It was the middle of the night, a red-eye flight with everyone snoring, scratchy blankets and thin, useless pillows wedged under necks, the galley curtains drawn so that even the flight attendants could get a few minutes of sleep, windows shuttered against the stars and all the twinkling that lay below. Cunning and dexterous Jane, in their two-seat row all the way in the back, who was no less nimble for being slightly drunk, was successful at being largely unseen. She got out of her seat and on the floor, in a position where she could stare up at him to invite him to make a decision. He nodded yes, accepting her silent offer, then closed his eyes like the other passengers. He said nothing—during, after. Did nothing in the moment beyond opening his legs slightly and stroking her head as she moved deftly under the thick, scratchy blanket that nearly smothered her, so she could have better access, so she could make sure he'd finish even if someone walked by.

Lucky for them, no one did. Also lucky, for Jane, that his member was far from outsized, and he was extremely discreet when he came, muffling his own groan with a large hand, as if he were only yawning. Then Jane wiped her mouth on the blanket, unseen, stood up and exited the row, washed up, redid her hair, and returned to find William sleeping. She followed suit, and what felt like soon afterward, the lights went on, and everyone was served one of those bizarre, twilight airplane breakfasts, a stale croissant and Turkish apricots three hours after their dinner of steak and Burgundy. As the food carts started coming down the aisle, Jane excused herself to go to the restroom for a second time, and on her return found William reading the *Financial Times*. "Good morning!" he brayed, not even giving her a wink.

Yet on the return flight from the conference to California, sitting in a different section of the plane from William, Jane found herself copied on all sorts of departmental emails and invited to participate in grant projects she knew nothing about, except that they were important for building a career. She got invited to department fundraisers, was asked to be the junior host for important speakers. Even other faculty, she felt, looked at her with the new respect accorded to a favorite and not the scorn she would have expected if he'd ever implied to anyone that she'd been, well, inappropriate—that catchall term for any deviant behavior, from nervous laughter at a formal research meeting, to impromptu blow jobs with no confirmatory words exchanged.

What surprised Jane at first was that he didn't seek to be physically close or even to travel alone with her again. There aren't any rumors about him, as there have been over the years about other, often younger male medical school faculty members known to date select medical students, like those with modeling experience. William has never been accused of dating or trying to date any trainees. His fairly athletic, competent-seeming wife is a poet too, like this annoyingly radiant medical student Renuka; Jane heard her telling William that once, talking about herself for no reason, absolutely none, with William looking interested. And even in the detailed progress and history notes that Renuka wrote, which, Jane was aware, had become even more carefully done since she started riding the poor girl, hazing her, really, making her pay for being treated as special—even in those medical notes, records of the patient's "subjective complaints," more like laments in some cases, Renuka did have a sensibility. William looked attentive when she says certain phrases. Ominous findings. A lesion of unexpected significance. Moribund. Edematous.

Had the plane episode happened? Had Jane only imagined sucking the great man? It was the wildest thing she'd ever done, an aberration that at times, she worried, meant she had desired or maybe even loved him all along and only discovered this when she sank down to her knees. She was sure they'd had their usual sort of flirtatious, muttered, sleepy conversation afterward about which women should and shouldn't still wear miniskirts and leather pants when they hit forty. His strong statement that Jane at forty would have the legs to wear whatever she liked. His singing softly, jokingly, that song from the musical, in response to her flattered expression, "People Will Say We're in Love." The newly awkward silence, she remembered, at the flight attendant's announcement that the cabin lights would be switched off and that they'd land in five hours, at which time William had arranged the blanket over Jane's lap as well as his own, as if being solicitous, touching her legs only slightly.

Jane's sliver of uncertainty about whether the sex act had in fact happened, a doubt that comforted her like warm light through a crack in a dirty window, was obliterated when, during the Christmas break immediately following their autumn plane trip, William and his wife invited her over for a roast and plum pudding. While the wife was finishing up preparing dinner in the kitchen, she, William, and a friend of his, someone from the neighborhood, were watching the game. Slightly tipsy from the combination of champagne, eggnog, and chilled white wine, Jane let a slew of curses fly out of her mouth when the quarterback on her hometown team fumbled. The neighbor, a mild-mannered widower in his seventies, looked rather stunned. William turned to her and laughed. Winked, saying to the neighbor, "Yes, our Jane has quite a mouth on her."

To make it all worse, this came at a time when Jane had become fed up with not having money. Silicon Valley in the early 2000s was a gold rush for the bold of heart. Obviously not for someone scrupulous and tame, like Renuka, whom Jane overheard last week, with one of her fellow medical students in the little atrium outside the onc unit, discussing the inequities of the dot-com revolution, the problems of the digital divide, drive-bys, and crack addicts in East Menlo Park. Charity was well and good, but—all in its place. Donations, charity galas, photogenic charity cases like children with cancer before the radiation got to them. Causes that built ties with senior faculty, the industry, conversations with titans in biotech and academia. These were pragmatic and grown-up causes Jane could celebrate. Not angry petitions, gritty protests, Occupy Wall Street and all that nonsense, Jane thought.

Of course, William was tickled by Renuka's social conscience, or at least, by her still seeming to have one. Engaged her, during rounds, in gentle and irrelevant debates on "what the sixties hippies ever accomplished." Nodded, serious, when she brought up the difficulties some refugee families had in paying for medication regimens and the uncertain housing status of a few older, concerningly fragile patients. Jane had even caught William watching Renuka when the girl wasn't aware of him, when she was at a bedside, for instance, nodding empathically at a patient's mother who was droning on, a rotund, warty Eastern European woman in shabby clothes, whose daughter had a slow-growing form of breast cancer, who visited bearing vats of soup, who was the butt of many jokes on the oncology service, particularly when rounds were early, and the fellows, residents, even the attending had had enough of Mrs. Ziolkowski's strong-smelling home remedies.

In front of Renuka, when William was the attending, he might say something serious, EmpathyBot-like: "It's important to support the family in feeling connected. It's right to help them keep up hope." And William was the first person to congratulate Renuka when she, before the residents, before even Jane and the fellows, correctly diagnosed a patient as having trismus: the sustained contraction of the jaw, painful and treatable, a complication of cancer treatment.

The most galling thing was that William would never lay a hand on Renuka. Her skin was smooth—unlined, untouched, her pursed ruby lips those of a virgin acolyte scribbling down William's words. Despite the near-daily tussles with Jane over how her script was written or whether Jane knew more details about radiation mucositis than some medical student (the girl read a ton, Jane gave her that)—despite all this, Renuka was going to get through unscathed, Jane just knew it. Even when matters escalated, when Renuka's composure broke upon hearing, from the nurses, about a patient who was complaining of incredible back pain, a potential cord-compression case, or even when Renuka the student dared to criticize Jane the attending physician in front of others, because Jane had taken a bit of time to come see the patient, had perhaps waited a couple of hours,

William did not shout at the annoying, self-righteous girl who took it upon herself to intervene, who seemed convinced that she was "good" while other doctors were only "going through the motions" or "trying to get away with what they could."

And by the way, there was no permanent consequence for the patient. He was dying anyway, Jane pointed out on rounds the next morning, expecting William's usual hearty chuckle, the dark medical humor that led to pearls of wisdom like, "Never diagnose what you can't treat." Jane was dismayed when, instead, he nodded and asked her if she had seen the spinal imaging. Which Renuka, it turned out, had called William after hours to ask permission to order, even though it wouldn't have changed the management of the case.

Renuka was working on the ward, devoted, while Jane was busy setting up her new Mountain View biotech consulting gig, going through a hard breakup, dealing with not having her first child by now like she always thought she would, interviewing potential new roommates, renegotiating rent, getting a massage, going running, for god's sake. Being a person. Renuka stayed after hours, vigilant, writing her excruciating, detailed notes, calling the attending, talking to every family member who looked sad, bringing cookies for the nurses, beaming when William praised her, while Jane plotted and fumed.

2.

Was there a way to stop Renuka cold? Jane's new roommate Derek, who had been living with her for three weeks, was the one who unexpectedly presented her with a possible solution, though she had known him only for exactly the same amount of time that Renuka, Derek's former med student, had been rotating on Oncology, with Jane.

Jane adores Derek. A vivacious, Spanish-fluent, foreign medical graduate, a gifted surgeon in training. He's the one who taught her about EmpathyBot. It's the running joke of the academic hospital surgery service, that the work life of a surgery resident, and even of a surgeon attending, would be much easier if there were a way to somehow get someone else to stand there nodding, listening, responding when patients express their terrors. To turf out to some entity, like to a robot, the demands of being present, being a kind listener, a responsive and reassuring witness, a perfect guide—even at the end of a thirty-hour shift or in the middle of a day of twenty hernia repairs, or, worst of all, on some day when one gets word from Patient Relations of "some sort of complaint" and can hardly breathe, trying to remember what, if anything, could have been unusual about the way one said goodbye to the patient the week before at the outpatient surgery clinic, what could have possibly led, Derek wondered with exasperation, to the person getting so offended they felt compelled to make their complaining, dumb calls. EmpathyBot, please, for the morbidly obese woman who's already had a lower extremity amputation and is saying that what she's most afraid of is losing her fingers, and can the surgeon promise, please, that if she tries to lose weight and quits smoking, she will keep her hands? EmpathyBot, even to take a seat in the chair at the patient's bedside, the seat that hasn't been used, which will never be used, because there's no one to visit or even bring this woman clean clothes, except for the doctor, who is there with a warm and understanding gaze at a respectful but humanizing distance, seated on the chair, nodding, answering questions, all patience, all pure connection. Only, in an ideal world, Derek likes to say, putting his feet up on the coffee table, too tired from his day to take off his scrub hat or prepare a drink, it would be the EmpathyBot sitting there in that musty, listless hospital room, the EmpathyBot that never gets cranky or tired or anxious, simply listening and listening, murmuring generic but specific enough reassurances to satisfy this patient, every patient, that the doctor sees him or her truly as individual.

"That's the problem," Derek concludes. "How to make what the bot says specific enough. How to make the bot dress and act classy enough too. So that it's better for medicine than, say, Jennifer Lopez was for Latin music. She's been trash. Really, nothing but trash. There are exquisite" (here he kisses his fingers) "mmhmmph, delicious women who can really sing. Not only Shakira, though she is a start. Why all the attention for la Lopez, a brown American, only a brown girl? She is low class. And does nothing for the image of Latin women."

Derek has a singular hatred for Puerto Ricans, Dominicans, island people—all mixed blood. Being from beautiful, imperial España himself, a young man from a family of noble, blue-eyed, respected academic surgeons in Madrid. Tall and trim doctors who all wore either immaculate scrubs or equally pristine, beautifully tailored tan suits and whose blue-black hair curled in the front like Superman's. Yet Derek now found himself with few choices, bogged down by what is called the transitional year, because he wasn't accepted into a regular five-year surgery program, perhaps on account of the rumor that dogged him from his previous transitional year that Derek lacked work ethic—the key point of pride for a surgeon, the one thing that would always, in Jane's opinion, make surgery training a lot more work than it was worth.

"There is this really pesky med student who kind of looks like Jennifer Lopez," Jane said, while drinking a good Chablis with Derek, days after Renuka started on the rotation, that girl with her textbooks and notebooks, who was already the topic of grateful whispers from nurses and techs for being around the ward at all hours, being willing to page the residents and attendings, even, when the nurses were worried or wanted their help but might have already asked and been dismissed by residents, attendings, busy adults. That girl who Jane had plans for, good plans, mean plans, justified plans.

Derek sat up at attention, nearly spilling his wine on the carpet, asking if the girl's name was Renuka, which he pronounced with such thoroughly entitled contempt that for a few seconds Jane truly envied him, knowing her own contempt would always be a form of affectation. And so, the story was uncorked, the details spilling out, intoxicating, delectable, with its own bouquet—Jane had learned that word not long before, from a wonderful wine trip to Napa— ready to be savored on the tongue. Ready to be converted from bad wishes and gossip to a specific plot against Renuka, "to destroy her," was the phrase Derek proposed, that Jane adopted willingly.

∽❧⁓

The story: Renuka was Derek's medical student on a cardiac surgery rotation. She was eager, hardworking, liked by the senior attendings, and willing to do all the scut work Derek's skill exempted him from (so he felt). Derek, for his part, was friendly, cheerful, honest, "and I gave her a wonderful experience, I thought, by letting her do so much." Yet Renuka, it turned out, complained to Derek's supervisor, the attending surgeon who ultimately was responsible to make sure Renuka was treated well, but who also had power over Derek's entire career. Apparently, Derek shared with disgust, Renuka had gone in tears to this attending, revealing that Derek had forced her to write endless postoperative and other progress notes, not actually teaching by giving her any information or showing her how to do any procedures, only using her to do the "grunt work" that was actually his legal responsibility as the person who operated. Derek was taken aside and spoken to, even disciplined informally, and now his prospects of "matching" into the academic surgery residency, indeed, into any surgery residency at all, had diminished.

His only saving grace? The power of his hands, the beauty of his work as a surgeon—his craftsmanship, pure love of it, efficiency, speed. On some level, all surgeons understood his desire to turf the scut in much the way that many of them would like to turf certain tasks to EmpathyBot. So all wasn't lost for Derek yet. He had been told that if he worked extra hard, and maybe even did a second transitional year, he still had a chance that coming spring to match into the academic hospital residency program. They still wanted him. He was still "one of the boys," a phrase that by the year 2000 had become equitable praise, the attendings were quick to point out. Derek's chief resident, after all, was a woman. Women were in charge of every arm of the academic hospital surgery program, and their ardor for surgery's long hours, their diligence, could quiet the men. If you were good enough, they always wanted you—like one of Derek's more senior colleagues, a young man from the Midwest who'd jeopardized everything by standing in a corner of the medical school library and pulling down his scrub pants to fondle himself in front of a particularly beautiful and sexy Korean American med student. But that young man was still deemed "the best neurosurgery candidate, bar none."

When Derek told that story, Jane, also Korean American, imagined the face of that woman. She wondered how she would have responded if the woman, the victim of the indecent exposure incident, the female med student, instead of a stranger, had been her sister. Though Jane had no siblings.

3.

Full of Derek's dishy details about Renuka, now armed with concrete evidence of the girl's betraying, conniving, insubordinate character,

her ability to dissemble obedience while still planning some disloy-
alty, such as going to an advising dean and complaining about the
rotation—complaining about William, Jane argued for the girl's de-
struction the next day, talking to William behind the closed door of
his office.

William for once looked somewhat startled and discomfited. He
would be up for associate chair in a few months. He couldn't afford
even a whiff of wrongdoing. Better to go to this girl's dean before
she could, William agreed with Jane, and without any resistance, not
even wincing a little at the thought of hurting Renuka, a fact that
Jane noted with satisfaction.

A discreet phone call—by William, not Jane. That was the most
Jane could get William to promise. As he led her out of his office,
hand pressing against the small of her back, Jane thought again of
their moment on the plane, the moment where, absent a known re-
ward, she gave him all. Now he would show his loyalty, maybe even
love. Now he would prove to Jane that she had the power.

The next day, Renuka was not on their team rounds. William,
carrying his clipboard and looking at the papers instead of at Jane's
face, was unexpectedly brusque, making Jane wonder if he regretted
carrying out the plan to bring down Renuka. To get her dean to put
something negative in the written record—a bad verbal evaluation, a
bad report, just bad, excluding Renuka from any but a bad residency
placement in some impoverished hospital.

But no one explained where Renuka was that morning. There
was no hint of gossip on the wards. There was a strange quiet in
Renuka's wake.

It was Jane who felt a moment of discomfort when, months later, she saw Renuka in the common room outside the main medical
school auditorium of the academic hospital, distributing flyers, along
with other Asians—Korean and Chinese Americans, as well as the

handful of foreign medical graduates fresh off the boat. The flyers were for free health screenings being offered to immigrant factory workers. Jane paused in front of their booth, smiled with high wattage, even made her calfskin leather Prada purse conspicuous, playing with the gold and ruby latches down the front, pretending that she might donate. But the young women weren't collecting donations, only trying to solicit volunteer physicians, residents, and medical students to carry out the health screenings, hands on. Renuka, who seemed taller and slimmer than Jane remembered, or perhaps was standing slightly straighter, impressively managed to avoid looking in Jane's direction at all. The two other women were also avoidant, conversing only with each other, although they were of East Asian descent, like Jane. "Second-generation Han Korean!" Jane felt like exclaiming but didn't.

Immediately after Jane got back to the oncology ward, she settled herself at the same workstation where she'd sat those tense weeks taunting Renuka. She had been warned by William never to stir up potential student complaints again, told sternly by him that she was not allowed to act so aggressively. Still, Jane went to the academic hospital's Internet directory, holding her breath to see whether Renuka was still counted as an "active med student" or maybe, if Jane were lucky, had been advised to take the offer of some kind of "leave," a strategy that the medical school, known for its gentleness and liberal attitude toward students, pursued when students were in danger of not getting a residency, to give them more time to balance any negative assessments with good ones.

If Renuka were finally gone, "dead" as a doctor, as it were, then Derek would feel incredible—Jane would be sure to let him know—and Jane might regain everything she'd worked so hard and sacrificed so much to get from William.

Ha. Yes. Renuka had taken a leave; at first this made Jane jubilant, since she, Jane, who hadn't read nearly as much, studied as much, or worked as long hours, had still been brilliant, savvy, and practical enough to finish on time, like everyone. Four years. But then Jane scrolled farther, and what she saw was not pleasing at all. Renuka had won some sort of scholarship to participate in community organizing, to increase Silicon Valley workers' access to preventive health. The dean of internal medicine himself awarded it, and this was how her leave was to be spent. To add insult to injury, Renuka was also involved in some kind of medical student "healing poetry" initiative. Renuka was photographed at some luncheon with William's wife, the published poet.

Jane realized she had been betrayed. It was William who must not have done what he and Jane planned together, or at least, not done it in a way that would have ended Renuka's career. William who wanted the good opinion of the dean. William who must have protected Renuka. Even without that brown girl getting on her knees.

Jane rallied, eyes narrowing in focus and anger. Jane then switched to a different website, where anyone could pretend to be a patient with a gripe against some bad doctor. All it would take was a few clicks—and Jane could tarnish, yes, even destroy, this girl forever. Post on the web, impersonating a patient. Call Renuka "cruel and dangerous," so that her patients, in the future, would approach her with distrust. Layered on top of the distrust they might already have toward "tricky foreigners." Expert, quick, always fast with her keyboard, given that useful minor in CS as an undergrad, Jane set up the fabricated but highly negative, even incendiary, assessment on the Internet, and was ready to click.

Too loud to ignore just then, Jane's pager went off. Code Blue. Decisive, Jane closed the whole false-assessment web page, canceled it in favor of the real. Assumed her position of authority, calling to the new med student to follow along so he would learn. Nodding at him in approval as he ran to keep up with her, as he told her the result of the latest imaging on the patient who was crashing now from the colliding tumors in his lungs, from the still oceans collecting inside him, from a gurgling silence that would rob him of his last words.

4.

Time passes.

5.

"Well, I guess we'll have to see how things turn out." It was Derek's supervisor, Tom, cardiac surgeon and amateur carpenter. An hour or so after Derek skillfully assisted on a long bypass, Tom offered to write him a letter. He stayed late in the OR, after everyone else left, standing, typing it up and printing it out on the computer on the countertop, placing it in an envelope. Then, holding it out, remembering how thrilled he was when he himself got into residency thirty years ago, the supervisor told a lengthy, grateful story about how he'd gotten in by the good luck of his medical school adviser going fishing with a good friend, the chair of surgery at the academic hospital.

"There's an old saying in Spanish, about how great men are able to chart their own destinies," said Derek, interrupting, impatient, wiping sweat off his brow with a bare hand, holding the same hand out for the letter. The supervisor sat down on a stool and let him take it, saluting him, muttering a sardonic, "Good luck."

"My God, Tom, you didn't really give our resident Speedy Gonzalez a letter?" asked the sharp nurse from the other side of the OR, once Derek left. She chuckled when he looked up at her. The supervisor knew her name not only from her badge but from the dirty text messages they'd spent a year exchanging after each of them had been divorced, before they each remarried other folks. "Shut your trap and come sit here," said the adviser, chuckling, patting his lap. She blew him a kiss, switched off the lights, went on her way, serene and unafraid of the pitch dark.

In a moment all the surgical overhead fluorescent lights were extinguished, except the small one beyond the doors of the OR, the overhead light in the vestibule where everyone had scrubbed in earlier in the day, and where Sam, Derek's new medical student, had spent the last productive hour learning the names of various tools from a kind OR tech who had been lining up and washing tools for nearly twenty years. To the tech, Sam already looked like a surgeon – so calm and confident, neat and handsome. So regular. Sam as it happened was a lanky sandy-blond scion of an old money family with its own healthcare foundation. Sam had known he was destined for orthopedic surgery since breaking his arm in a rugby game at boarding school, since watching a sports surgeon at a regatta when he was twelve. Sam found it easy enough to tune out most of what was said by Derek, who constantly complained about the surgical residents' workload, but didn't quite dare to force this six-foot-three blond handsome heir, who reminded him so much of that famous, rugged Mexican actor, Sergio Sendel, to do all his work for him.

When the lights inside the OR went off, the OR techs recognized the darkness as a signal to go eat dinner, and quickly left, but the calm student Sam stayed where he was, at the sink, carefully washing and rewashing his hands. The value of these hands of his, considered over his lifetime, was infinite, Sam thought, with gratitude and, he thought, humility. Often he gave thanks for them, these hands. Large, dusted with white-blond hairs, the nails precisely cut, the fists of great power and grace, though since deciding on ortho, at age ten, Sam avoided fistfights and woodworking, as a precaution. Sometimes, in the early dawn, no later than 4 am, when he started his day by thrusting into the very pretty undergrad girl he lived with, instead of looking at her unmade-up, rosy face, he stared at his own hands pressing into her shoulders.

∽◉∽

In January 2000, thousands of lights prick the night around the Golden Gate Bridge, peak of the dot-coms, lights sparkling on a bubble growing larger and larger, floating weightless and skirting the inevitable. Lights wash in the night over the supplicant faces of devout Catholics who gather to listen to Pope John Paul II, beloved, apologizing for past wrongdoings by the Catholic Church, including the widespread, heretofore-unpunished sexual abuse of innocents. The Tate Modern Gallery opens, one installation made of curlicues of costly neon lights.

In Sierra Leone, civil war, amputations, sudden and painful infectious and non-infectious deaths. Emergency surgeons are required, along with equipment like makeshift surgical tents, sharps, cases of medicine, portable overhead lights. Sam volunteers with a Catholic charity mission, collects these donations beforehand. Is killed when his jeep drives over an IED to reach Masanga Hospital. Then at Stanford Main hospital a few months later: a plaque commemorating him, speeches describing Sam as a true American hero, an example for everyone. Assad becomes the leader of Syria. The ILOVEYOU computer virus is discovered to have originated in the Philippines, prompting waves of early anti-Asian hate. In Hampshire, the United Kingdom, outside the house of a known pedophile, riots, protests, people carrying posters showing the shadows of children, victims who haven't had a chance to speak.

Derek, eating a bowl of cheap noodles one day post-call, at 9 a.m., turns on the TV and doesn't move for two hours, watching and laughing at the Spanish-English bilingual educational cartoon show *Dora the Explorer,* the characters reminding him of tantes and abuelas back home, of his nieces. He's drawn the curtains of his Mountain View studio closed to block out the morning light. It isn't really lonely. Still, he texts Jane, who is still his good friend though not a roommate, telling her they should meet up for dinner, shrugging when she texts back *can't* and a sad face, followed by *have to work.* Derek texts back heart emojis, mutters *Trabajar duro,* knowing neither he or Jane can take anything they have for granted.

Charlatans claim to have found and dug up a Persian mummy princess in Pakistan, her face exquisitely preserved, a girl who must have been favored. In a temperate December 2000, Florida, Gore stops the recount, surrendering the presidency to Bush. A few short months later, the world will know about the Enron debacle, and in the interim the Bush dynasty, protecting its wealth against such scandals, transfers vast sums to Saudi business partners, members of the bin Laden family.

2001 brings colder lights. September is indelible, small blinking lights on monitors, signalling lights for airline towers, futility. The first plane crashes into a building, decimates, while thousands of second-year medical students study for Step I of their national board exams; groggy in the morning, watching lecture videos with a cut screen to CNN for daily news, then watching only the news with rising nausea, hands on their mouths.

In later hours, dread, mourning, and lights blinking through ash. Early wreaths placed in hopeless clearings, making urban shrines. Anger as demanding as grief. Anger that's clamoring louder.

Renuka, visiting friends at Harvard, is walking through a part of Somerville that intersects an old Italian and a newer Portuguese neighborhood, when a young child not more than nine years old is shouting from a passing car, suddenly, insisting, "Back to your country, you fucking Paki!"

It is oddly comforting that in Seattle, where Renuka interviews after that day for residencies in general surgery, people still admire the nine-foot black monolith in the city center created by a mysterious artist. No one has ascribed it to terror, or other malicious intentions. The top of it looks as sharp and polished as any scalpel. The city received it as a gift.

∾◉෴

Two years later: Jane is working for a large pharmaceutical company about an hour away from the academic hospital where she first met William. She is advancing quite quickly. She no longer needs William's approval, or even sees him very much; her new boss is a charming white man younger than William and much more professional. He does nothing except give her a few lingering looks. She doesn't have time for dating, likes being single. Derek, still her roommate, has performed nearly fifty appendectomies, all of them flawless. He's reconciled to never being chief resident but knows he'll earn a great living. He still abuses med students, although one or two of them he's taken to lunch, and the daughter of a family friend from home, who *looks like Shakira,* Jane teases him, via text, is coming to study surgery in the US, and will benefit from his advice.

But Renuka is gone, graduated or flunked out, Jane has no idea where she is now. Her name and picture don't show up on any internal medicine residency websites, and occasionally, when Jane looks her up, she fantasizes that in spite of William's benevolence, Renuka's at once anxious and stubbornly perfectionistic attitude made it impossible for her to graduate, and now she's trying to find a job outside medicine. Jane enjoys picturing Renuka as fat, exhausted-looking, depressed from too many failures. Alone, a visible loser. Maybe she couldn't cut it, Jane imagines. Hopefully, Renuka, unlike Jane, will soon be without friends and out of money.

But Jane still monitors the academic medical school newsletters, just in case. She does web searches for Renuka's name in other specialties. She stays alert when William takes her out to lunch once every few months, wondering now, not if he'll ever bring up what Jane gave him, so unselfishly, on the plane eight years ago, but if William will bring up Renuka, and maybe share some news of her success. Because Jane Chun, MD and soon to be a pharmaceutical CMO, has learned this much from all the training she's received in medicine: It is nearly impossible to destroy a person.

THE DEVIL'S DOORBELL

AMANDA LEDUC

T HE DEVIL COMES TO me one night when I am almost asleep, staring out the window as the sirens wail outside. They always wail here, deep in the heart of the city, though not for the reasons you might think. Nana says they come to take away the old people who give out in the middle of the night. Stopped hearts, an aneurysm exploding in an octogenarian brain like the smallest burst of bloody stars.

I've never heard a gun here where Nana lives, so she's probably right. It makes me think about how, if ambulance sirens are so prevalent—if *death,* normal old *death,* is so prevalent here, if we hear it all the time—then everyone who lives away from the city must be doing something wrong. Ignoring it. Pretending it doesn't happen.

Nana says she doesn't even hear the sirens anymore, she's so used to it. She has a whole drawer in the hallway side table that's full of blank condolence cards. All she has to do is wait for a neighbor to tell her that So-and-So from two streets over has passed away, and she has a card whipped out and ready to go.

So Sorry For Your Loss.

Thinking of You.

Thoughts Are With You In This Difficult Time.

Except they aren't, not really, because Nana just fills out the card and walks over to pop it in someone's mailbox and then goes about her day. At night, she has no trouble sleeping.

Me, I lie awake. The sirens throb in my ears and pound in my feet for hours.

On the night the Devil comes, my hands are tangled in the sheets and the slickness of my flesh and the pain in my feet is just a low tingle, finally. My body a vehicle for pleasure as well as pain. There... there...*there*. I cry out. Then there's a knocking at the window and when I look up, there she is. Finally. She waves at me and smiles.

I've never seen her before, and yet I know who she is. I swing my legs over the side of the bed, Nana's old nightgown brushing the tips of my curled, crooked toes, press up and on my feet and limp across the floor to the window, opening it up, letting her in.

"Took you long enough," I say. Nana would think I'm being rude, but the Devil only smiles.

"Took *you* long enough," she says. "I know six-year-olds who can masturbate better than you."

"I'm out of practice," I say, because it's the truth. Sort of. I haven't really practiced before at all, thanks to Nana.

The Devil laughs. She is young; younger than I'd expected the Devil to be. Mid-twenties, maybe a little older. I wonder if she drives.

"Sure I drive," she says, and then she laughs. "You want to go for a spin?"

"You have a car?" It's all I can think to say.

The Devil shrugs. "I have whatever I want," she says. "Everything belongs to me." Then she nods at my feet. "You should lie back down," she says. "Your feet hurt. I can feel them from here."

I don't ask her how she knows this; I just go back to the bed. The Devil follows me and helps me back onto the mattress. Her hands are warm and gentle. She wears a gauzy blue shirt and smart black leggings, strappy black stilettos that make me simmer with want. I stretch my legs out—my feet are throbbing again with the sirens. Too much walking today, too much noise.

"You're in pain," the Devil says, and her hand traces the arch of my scarred and twisted foot. Where her fingers touch, a warmth spreads. "Let me help you."

"Yes," I say, because why not. If this is a dream, I'll probably forget it in the morning.

Even though I know it isn't really a dream.

But her hand leaves my foot and travels higher, her fingertips trailing along my calf, moving up beneath the hem of Nana's horrid nightgown, along my thigh. Higher still, slow and lovely, until they cup the damp triangle of my underpants. She looks at me, an eyebrow quirked.

It's all I can do to nod.

In the morning, when she comes downstairs with me for breakfast, Nana takes one look at her—at us—and knows.

∽◉∾

At school, the Devil carries my books for me like a perfect lady. Everyone knows who she is, even Mr. Higgins, the science teacher, who has spent hours in front of us saying that the Devil, and God, do not exist at all.

"Mr. Higgins," the Devil says smoothly, when they lock eyes in the hall.

Mr. Higgins flushes to the red roots of his hair. He looks like a giant human beet. "Ah," he says. "Ah." He clears his throat. "I didn't know. Forgive me."

The Devil flashes a smile. "What's to forgive?" she says gaily. "You spread my work and you don't even know it." She reaches over and clasps Mr. Higgins's arm. The teacher looks down, startled, as though surprised that the Devil's hand is only a hand. The nails smooth and pearlescent. No claws.

She follows me into every class and holds my hand across the desk. No one tells her she isn't allowed. Why would they? *How* could they? The Devil gets into everything, just like Nana says. Instead everyone tries to avoid eye contact, which only sort of works. I watch them all stand straighter, clear their throats, project their voices. As though the superintendent has come to give everyone reviews.

In second-period English, she raises her hand and then interrupts as Ms. Malcolm reads to us from the Brothers' Grimm.

"You've got the wrong version of the story," she says. "The father cut her hands off first."

We are reading "Maiden Without Hands," which tells of how a good and pious maiden is traded away to the Devil by her father in exchange for gold and riches.

"I didn't do that," the Devil insists. "Her father wanted to take her to bed. When she refused, he told her her hands were evil. Then he cut off her hands and her breasts and made her walk the world a beggar. *I* gave her silver hands to help her survive."

Ms. Malcolm clears her throat. "This is the seventh edition of the book," she says. Her voice apologetic. "We might have…we might have read that story had we looked for an earlier edition."

"Look for it," the Devil says. Her voice as smooth as glass again, her hand around mine warm and sure. "I won't have you telling everyone lies."

◦◦◦

At lunch, she sits across from me at my corner table and watches smugly as everyone lines up to take a seat. No one's avoiding eye contact now.

"Call me Max," she says as they approach. And then, when they get even closer, "Fuck off. We don't need you here." She steals a glance at me again and reaches for my hand. "I don't need anyone else," she tells me. "You'll always be enough for me, Meg."

No one has ever said this to me, not even my own mother. Not even Nana.

Nana, with her pink cheeks and horrified frown in the kitchen. *What have you done, Meg? What have you done?*

But people ignore her, keep on coming even as she continues to send them away. They cannot help it. They are as drawn to her as I am.

Are they as desperate for her? No. No one else summoned the Devil from their bare and lonely bedroom. That was all me.

Pretty soon Ms. Malcolm comes to stand in front of us. She's pushing a girl in a wheelchair, someone I've never seen before.

"Meg," Ms. Malcolm says to me. She doesn't look at Max. "Meg, this is Ingrid."

Ingrid lolls her head at me and smiles a crumpled smile. Her left eye looks up to the heavens; the other one looks directly at me.

I hold my breath and look at Max; when she doesn't say anything, I let my breath go and roll my eyes.

"Let me guess, Ms. Malcolm. Ingrid is new and doesn't have any friends and you thought I could be friends with her because I'm a cripple too." The words taste sweet, like strawberries.

Ingrid flinches; Ms. Malcolm shakes her head and looks at the floor. "That's not—that's not what I mea—"

"It's always what you mean," I say. Max's hand around my own grips tighter, warmer. *Good girl,* I hear her say somewhere. *You let her have it.*

Ms. Malcolm clears her throat. "I brought her over because I thought—I thought you might understand one another, Meg. That's all."

"*I* don't use a wheelchair," I snap. I'm almost shouting. The cafeteria is frozen, silent, heavy. "I don't know anything *about* using a wheelchair. I walk just like a *normal* person. I don't know what you're talking about!"

No one points out that I'm lying. They don't see the folded cane that sits snugly in my backpack. They might have seen me use it on a bad day, but no one brings this up. They see my twisted feet—no one brings this up either. The Devil sits right across from me, holding my hand.

Ms. Malcolm nods. Ingrid looks almost bored, like she expected this; Ms. Malcolm looks like she's going to cry. "I'm sorry," she whispers. "I won't make this mistake again." Then she wheels Ingrid in a circle and pushes her away.

∽◎∼

In the girls' bathroom, the yellow OCCUPIED cone outside in front of the door. Max's lips against the inside of my thigh, her fingers higher, my jeans puddled around ankles on the floor. I'm late for fourth period; I don't even care.

"The story," I gasp out, and Max laughs so hard my legs shake, which is probably why I do it. "Did you really give her silver hands? The version we read said those came from the king."

In the story, the Maiden Without Hands is forced to go out into the world, subsisting on charity. But then she meets the king and falls in love. He gives her a pair of silver hands that work just like her old ones.

"It's a fairy tale," Max says. She pulls my panties down and plants a kiss. Not on my thigh this time. "I can give her anything you want, Meg. Just like I can give you anything you want."

What I want. The Ms. Malcoms and the Mr. Higgins of the

world crushed beneath the force of their own pity. Like ants beneath
the heel of my shoe.

Even Ingrid, I think, as Max touches my insides with her tongue.
Even Ingrid, who held a weird kind of pity in her uneven eyes as Ms.
Malcolm turned her in a circle and pushed her away. Ingrid can go
beneath my shoe along with everyone else.

After, as I zip up my jeans and smooth down my top and get ready
to go back to class, I watch Max watch me and try to tamp down the
niggling feeling in my gut. "Why here," I ask her. "Why me."

Meg, Nana said to me that morning. Her voice urgent and shrill.
Meg, you must stop this right now. She's here because you asked *for her.
You summoned her in. Tell her to leave us* at once!

As if I didn't know. As if I hadn't been trying to do exactly that.

The Devil only shrugs. "Why not you?" she asks. "Why can't you
be special and worthy of all the world's attention?"

But even this feels wrong, somehow. I am used to feeling special,
in the bad way—extraneous, superfluous, a burden. The person who
stays quiet in order to blend into the wall. If people don't notice you,
they don't notice how you walk, or what you need, or whether and
how the things that you need might be different from the needs of
someone else.

If people don't notice you, they won't laugh at you for needing
any of these things.

"I'll never wear stilettos," I tell her. "I'll never be—pretty—in the
way that you deserve."

"You've been listening to your Nana too much," she says. Her
voice is dark, and not in the sexy kind of way. "Fuck her and whatever prayers she rode in on."

I laugh. I cannot stop laughing. On the other side of the bathroom door, my knees wobble and give out. Max catches me as though
I weigh nothing. I straighten.

"I'm okay," I say, instantly, although what I really want to say is *let's blow this joint and disappear.* Instead we go to class and walk into the room hand in hand. The cripple and the devil. No one says anything; two students even vacate their seats at the front of the room and we sit there. The eyes of my classmates a hot pressure on the back of my head for the rest of the hour.

∽☙∾

We skip fifth period entirely and walk back to my house, where Nana is sitting tearful with the police at the kitchen table.

Max looks at everyone. She's still holding my hand. "Officers?" she asks, as though she's done something wrong.

The officers look to Nana, then clear their throats. "We've received a report," the first one says.

"On what?" Max asks.

"Well." The officer blushes. I'm sure he didn't wake up thinking today was going to be the day he blushed in front of the Devil, but there you go. "On you, ma'am."

The Devil smiles, then squeezes my hand. "*Ma'am,*" she says. "I like that. But I don't *actually* believe I've done anything wrong, Officer."

"She is taking a *child* away from me!" Nana shouts. "She was up *in her room* all of last night."

"I'm not a child, Nana," I say.

"You are *sevent—*"

"Soon to be eighteen," Max interrupts. She nods at the officers. "The legal age of consent here is sixteen, last time I checked." She glances back at me. "Also, last time I checked—the *child* here does not appear to be in any distress."

The officer clears his throat again. "Yes. Well—ah. Ma'am—" and he nods to Nana—"You see, the law here is clear. There's not really anything we can do."

"She doesn't know her own mind!" Nana shrieks.

"I think Meg knows her own mind quite well," the Devil says. "After all, she let me in, Officers. She called me, and I came."

In the silence that follows, I feel the officers' embarrassment expand beyond the house. *Jesus Christ,* I hear them thinking. *When will this goddamned day be over.*

The younger of the officers clears his throat and looks at me. "Ah—is this true, ma'am?"

I blink at him, at Nana. "Is *what* true, Officer?"

"Did you, ah, *summon*…the other party."

"I didn't draw a pentagram on my floor, if that's what you're asking."

"Oh for *heaven's* sake, Meggie." Nana wrings her hands. "I told you. I told you! I told you that your—that your body is the Devil's instrument."

"That's not what you said, Nana. Tell them what you said."

She glances at the officers, then blushes. "The clitoris," she whispers. "The clitoris is the Devil's doorbell, Meggie. You touch it, you invite him in."

In the silence that follows, I hear one of the officers stifle a snicker.

"Is that true," the other one says to me.

I shrug. "I don't know, Officer. What do *you* think of when you jerk off at night?"

"Meggie!" Nana shrieks.

"Last I checked," Max says smoothly, "I don't look very much like a *he,* do I."

"She is—she is the Devil!" Nana wails. "She has *seduced* her with promises of—of a life that she can't have."

My hand in Max's tightens, throbs. "And what would that life be, Nana? One so different from the life here with you, in my nightgown, forever?"

"Oh Meggie, don't be so *dramatic,*" she implores. "I want you to be well. And safe. That's all I've ever wanted for you. You know that."

I do. I think of the condolence cards gathered in her hall table, Nana so blithely sending out *sorrys* to families of the friends who've departed after safe, predictable lives. Like the card she sent to my own mother, once upon a time. After learning about my diagnosis, but before Mom had left.

Thoughts Are With You In This Difficult Time.

As though my life had ended with one diagnosis. My safe, predictable, here-is-the-world-where-Meggie-grows-up-to-run-a-marathon life. And now here we were, contemplating a life with my twisted body the same way you contemplate life when someone's died.

I tighten my grip around the Devil's hand. The heat from her palm seems...otherworldly. Which I guess just makes sense when you think about it.

"I *am* well," I say. "And I've never been safer."

"Meggie," Nana whispers. But that's all she gets out. When Max turns to go, still holding my hand, I spare one last glance for the three of them, clustered around the table. Then I turn and follow Max out the door, into the world.

I should have summoned her sooner.

AMARANTH

LAUREN GROFF

S HE WAS TWELVE WHEN her father died; she was round, downy, tiny in her bones.

She smiled shyly and constantly, an only child with busy parents. Her name was Amaranth. They called her Merry.

She was in the backseat of the car, dozing, when it happened. Her hair was wet from swim practice, her body lax. Her father had a phone call and his voice went loud. When the car stopped, she saw that they were at his business partner's slick glass apartment building downtown. Amaranth was still half sleeping when she saw her father opening the car door, Otto in his purple robe and pajamas running out of his building. She saw the dawn sky, cherry shading to gold.

There was nobody on the ice of the sidewalk but the two men, meeting.

There was a shout. Otto's palm suddenly extended and then her father arced backward through the spangled air, his arms spread in a reverse swan dive. She saw him land. He lay still on the ground, and a black puddle grew around his head.

She saw. She'd seen. What? She told nobody. She carried her seeing in her arms like a dangerous and napping creature, through the service in the soaring white church, through the gathering in their house afterward, that pale forest of adult faces. The Christmas decorations had been hurriedly put away, a solitary angel stranded on the mantel. Family friends came in, one after another, like jet beads on a string. The snow melted on their shoulders, they crouched to embrace Amaranth. When too many came, she carried what she had seen up to her room all aflower, cabbage roses on the curtains, forget-me-nots on the dust ruffle, pink roses someone had sent that morning in cloying bloom on her dresser. She lay on the floor and felt the vibrations in the frame of the house as the front door opened and closed, opened and closed, and the guests who had come in finally escaped back out to the dim gray afternoon.

When the house went silent, there was her mother in the gloom of the doorway, tall and black-haired, her face a perfect oval, tears in her lashes. Oh, Merry, her mother whispered, and opened her arms. With a shiver, Amaranth went in.

∽

But in the middle of the night she left her mother sleeping in her parents' enormous bed, with its perplexing odors and its hard pillows.

We die; we leave ghosts of ourselves behind. Voices on answering machines, bodies on video, fragments of souls in handwriting. A cold north wind blew the windows to rattling; a bell in the garden rang a frantic steady ring. If Amaranth gathered up all the tiny pieces of her father's ghost and focused hard enough, he could return to her. He could tell her what to do with her new, nipping suspicions. In his closet, purged of clothes, she taped up his photographs, she smelled his favorite sweater, she hunched over his laptop and watched clips of him until she slept.

Her father urging baby Amaranth to walk, his arms outstretched.

Her father giving an interview on a news magazine about excessive Wall Street bonuses, his nervous tic, a tap at the nosepiece of his glasses.

Her father running alongside Amaranth on a bicycle beside the pond at the country house. Plump and laughing, pushing her forward, picking her up when she falls, taking off her enormous pink helmet, kissing the crown of her hurt head while she cries. Smiling up at the camera as he holds her, says, Patience, honey.

The wind howled. The snow turned to ice, scratched at the windows. She waited. Before dawn, she felt her father's hands on her face, his breath on her ear, saying, Patience. Gather your power. Distract. Collect.

When she reached out, he was gone.

She was left with, what? A riddle. She kicked in fury at the laptop and split the screen neatly from the keyboard. She was still clutching the dead screen in her hands when her mother found her curled up and sleeping in the closet the next morning.

∞

She was lost, confused. A month slid by and Amaranth did nothing. Her mother was in and out of the house all day, the lawyers calling, the housekeeper Rosalie helping Amaranth with homework because her mother was too busy. Amaranth fell asleep every night in her mother's bed, woke to her mother's body stretched beside hers.

Then she began waking in her own bed, her mother carrying her back when she came in at night. After a week of such hinting, Amaranth gave up going to bed in her parents' room and fell asleep in her own.

One day she woke in the dark predawn to the front door closing and shaking the house. She rolled to the window and saw Otto's white-blond head, his glasses shining in the streetlight as he hurried down the sidewalk. When she went to the kitchen, her mother was already there, spatula in hand, pancakes on a plate, robe cinched, lipsticked. Rosalie was the one who made breakfast. Her mother slept until nine. Amaranth ate the pancakes and watched her mother and when she finished her last bite, she understood what Otto had been doing there so early.

∽⊘∼

Amaranth had stopped swimming: her father had been the one to take her to morning practice. She became quiet in school. She was thinking. Distract, he had said. Collect. She wrote the words in tiny letters on the sole of her shoe.

Murmurs reached her. Her mother was selling their part of the hedge fund to Otto. She would retain a seat on the board. Amaranth's family hadn't ever worried about money, but now they truly would never worry again. Her mother came home one day with tulip bulbs and sang when she put them into the little garden behind the brownstone, though they had a gardener to do all that, and she had never sung before, even in the shower. Winter turned to spring and the tulips did not come up.

One night, Otto came to dinner, bringing Thai, Amaranth's favorite, in white shopping bags. He pulled her to his lap, his face in her hair, his smell of wool and coffee and cigar. He had always been there, every holiday, every family trip; he was the one who manned the barbecue at the country house in the summer. Amaranth's father and Otto had been college roommates. He hugged her tightly and she looked up to see his eyes filling behind their glasses, tears leaking out at the corners. She moved to her own seat and pretended to eat. She listened to her mother and Otto talk, comforting half sentences, his words clipped, hers soft. She glanced up to find them flushed, lingering, in love. Her suspicions were either goaded or soothed; she wouldn't know until later.

Amaranth choked on her loneliness in the seat between them.

At last, her mother said, Merry, go to bed. You have school in the morning. Amaranth left the room; Otto stayed.

Amaranth kept the light off, thinking of her mother and Otto downstairs. She undressed in the mirror, looked at her goosepimpled body. She was small, tub-like, her chin soft and round. An underlayer of plump. There was no power in her, yet.

Distract, she thought. Until there is.

∽

Begin small. Begin subtle. Live on oranges and air.

When her mother noticed that Amaranth had lost weight, she laughed with pleasure and bought her a new dress. She crowed to her friends about how beautiful Amaranth was becoming. Look at my baby, she said. Growing up.

It took months to burn off the baby fat. Amaranth's wrist bones showed; her eyes in her face were enormous. Her mother frowned, looking at her one morning; something in her face went still. She took her after school to the ice cream parlor, but Amaranth only mashed the ice cream into the banana. She took her to a doctor, a jovial Indian fellow with pointed eyebrows and white streaks in his beard. Amaranth would not talk; she and the doctor gazed at one another during the sessions until her eyeballs went dry.

She didn't realize he had a British accent until their fourth session, when he sent Amaranth out and asked to speak with her mother; she listened at the door, biting her lips at how very serious their voices sounded. Her mother's forehead grew deep wrinkles, which she had to have surgically smoothed. Her mother took Amaranth to the hairdresser's to do something about her newly brittle hair and she came out with a sleek bob that made her look even bonier.

It wasn't that she wasn't tempted; she was. A Yorkshire pudding, a meatloaf, a pain au chocolat, a turkey, a fourth of July barbecue at the country house, Otto in an apron painting sauce on ribs.

He made her virgin daiquiris; he made her his German potato salad, which she had once loved so much she'd eaten it until she was sick. At the pond in the afternoon, he split a watermelon on a boulder. It was the exact sound of her father's head against the sidewalk.

If he flushed a little, only Amaranth noticed.

Her mother's friend Julie gasped when she saw Amaranth in her bathing suit. She pulled her close, said, oh, Merry, you *have* to start eating, you're just a bundle of twigs. But Amaranth shrugged her away, and went into the pond, and had to work just to stay afloat. She watched the relentless fat bellies of the clouds drift past.

In the mornings now, there were chalky drinks concocted for old bodies. Her mother at her feet, reading the scale. A fine light fuzz on Amaranth's arms. The precise calculations to hover near hospitalization, just a breath above.

For her thirteenth birthday, they bought her a violin, as if music could make her hungry. She loved it for its immoderate screech, its sob, all she wouldn't do.

She overheard her mother weeping on the telephone to the doctor. She's a very, very sick little girl, her mother said. She's going to stunt her growth! But he said something to calm her, he made her stop crying, he made her laugh; men loved to make her mother laugh. Besides, there was no immediate danger. Amaranth's report cards were perfect, although she no longer spoke in school. Her old friends had faded away first in embarrassment and then in disgust. She didn't miss them; friends were inessential. She burned, white-hot, alone.

Amaranth watched her mother and Otto mistaking her body, spun of sugar and gristle, for an essential frailty in the girl herself. Good, she thought. Let them.

To his credit, the doctor did not. After over a year of silence, he talked. There is something deeper going on, Amaranth, he said, pursing his lips. You have walked a knife's blade admirably for a very long time without having fallen over. I think you are making a point, but I don't know what point it is. Please. I ask you, tell me.

On the tip of her tongue: *I saw*. But she couldn't. There was an engine inside her; if exposed to air, it would rust, it would flake away, bit by bit.

∾

Two years and a day after her father died, her mother and Otto quietly got married. They went to city hall. Her mother wore silver raw silk. They told Amaranth at night by pouring her a glass of champagne. She smiled very brightly and when they weren't looking, she tipped her champagne over as if by accident and sat watching them scurry to mop it up. They kissed when their hands met on the paper towels. Amaranth felt their happiness like a hot wind against her face.

Her mother and Otto went to Japan on their honeymoon and left Rosalie to watch over Amaranth. To keep Rosalie from feeling hurt, Amaranth ate five small bites of whatever the housekeeper made each night: enchiladas, stuffed shells, quinoa salad, baked flounder. Healthy! Rosalie said, Good girl! and Amaranth laughed and put her head on Rosalie's shoulder and Rosalie sat down and held her so tightly Amaranth couldn't move.

For two weeks, all was calm. Then her mother and Otto returned, glowing, and Otto moved in.

You don't have to call me Dad, Otto said shyly in his turquoise

Japanese reading glasses. You can call me anything.

She grinned at him, and he waited for her to speak, and when it was clear she wouldn't, he said with a little plangent note in his voice, To be sure, I've always wanted to be called Papa. I like Papa. It is what I called my father. What do you think?

She nodded but wouldn't call him by any name. You, she called him. Him, she called him. He.

∞◎∽

Amaranth was fourteen when they sent her to summer camp, a euphemism for this convocation of bones. Girls like crows, with pointy beaks and ribs and knees. Girls who'd shatter in a slight wind.

Amaranth ate what they told her to. She swam when the others swam. She rode the horses, loving the jolt to her joints as she posted. Her roommate, a girl who had once been a piano prodigy, stopped getting out of bed and they sent her off somewhere and Amaranth was alone in her white nun's cell. You're doing so good, Merry! the camp director said, patting Amaranth's head whenever she saw her plate emptied. Keep it up!

It was her new strategy, compliance: she would come home looking healthier, ten pounds heavier, sun-browned, hair glossed. She would lull them into thinking she was better. Patience. She'd let them relax. Then she would scare them.

But they were the ones who surprised her. By the time she returned in September, they'd sold the brownstone, the country house, Otto's apartment. Make a clean slate of it, Amaranth's mother said, turning the car down a long gravel drive lined in poplars. Start anew, without any old memories dragging us down.

By any old memories, Amaranth knew, her mother meant her father. By clean slate, she meant to banish more remnants of his ghost.

No more pond where he'd taught his daughter to swim. No more swing in the willow he'd made with his own hands. She hadn't had a chance to say goodbye.

I hate you, she said, but so softly her mother said, What? They had pulled up to a vast stone house. Otto in the passenger seat chuckled in anticipation. There was a barn, a greenhouse, a river curling beyond. What did you say, Merry? her mother said, frowning.

Nothing, she said.

Her mother said, Well. Well, we bought you a mare, and closed the car door and led Amaranth into the barn, and the girl put her hand up to the damp, soft nose of a sorrel that snuffled and sneezed in her palm, and her mother's pinched face softened to see her daughter laughing.

In the night, Amaranth walked over the lawn, by the perennial gardens, down to the river. She turned and looked at the broad stretch of the house, the stables, the greenhouse glimmering in the moonlight. She would douse it all in kerosene, she would torch it all. She saw before her a screaming horse alight, galloping toward the black river; she saw her mother and Otto in their beds in the morning, lumps of greasy charcoal.

They had upped the ante. Well, now. Amaranth could see. She could raise.

∽◎∽

She bought a straight razor from an old-timey haberdasher's. For my dad, she told the natty little man who sold it to her, with his bowtie, his tapered chin, and he blinked and nodded, but still looked worried.

She made an experimental cut and watched as the peroxide bubbled and subsided. For a few months, she waited. Her doctor stared at her mistrustfully: You have a new energy, he said. New energy makes me nervous.

Her mother had slowly involved herself again with her boards and taking tennis lessons in town. She had a subtle filling injected in her lips and cheekbones. It was a good year for the hedge fund, Otto had said, and for Christmas he bought Amaranth's mother a three-strand diamond necklace. Darling! her mother shouted, and called Rosalie in to see it. Her mother draped it on Amaranth's neck and it felt heavy, armor-like, cold. For Amaranth there was a pearl on an insipid gold chain.

A few days after her fifteenth birthday, Amaranth struck. She wore her mother's white cashmere sweater to dinner and not enough gauze. By the time the steamed chicken and broccoli was served, she saw the red weeping through the weave. She reached for the pitcher of ice water slowly, slowly, and her mother's face blanched. She grabbed Amaranth's arm, she ripped the sleeve up, she burst into tears when she saw her daughter's bloodied arm.

And then her mother, tall, fit, held her daughter down, took off Amaranth's clothes right there, as if she were an infant, looked and looked at her daughter's body, a frame of bones with a canvas of skin. Otto stood at the head of the table, napkin held to his mouth. Rosalie in the doorway pressed her face between her hands. Amaranth lay, watching the hatred move over her mother's face, then the fear, and then relief when there was only a single previous puckered scar.

In the night, the doctor arrived and drove them all to the private hospital. Her mother cried and cried in the front seat to the doctor's cooing noises, and in the back, Otto put his hot hand on Amaranth's as if to give her comfort, as if to silently press into her his love.

∽⚬∾

The hospital was clean, quiet, a broad lake of window light. She finished her sophomore-year schoolwork three months early. She turned sixteen. She sat in group meetings in which she listened to the other girls' tiny, endlessly plucked problems. They were flies, inconsequential; it took all Amaranth's strength to keep from swatting them. She said what she was supposed to say and in private fed the living thing inside her, soothed it, groomed it. Midsummer, her mother picked her up and held her for a long time and Amaranth saw with a surge of pleasure the deep creases by her eyes, Otto's hair gone white at the temples.

Her mother took her to the beach, just the two of them: girls' weekend! Amaranth spoke of the future in clinic-speak: Acceptance and Courage to Change and Surrender. Her mother drank a whole bottle of wine and leaned forward and talked about her own sadness when her own parents died, and said, You won't always feel this sad, Merry. You'll grow and go to college, and be happy again.

Amaranth shrugged and said, College, well. Except I won't get in? She'd learned from the other girls to lilt the end of her sentences, defanging them.

Her mother laughed. What are you talking about? she said. You have perfect grades and PSATs. You'll have perfect SATs, too.

But Amaranth said, I have no extracurriculars? and savored the way her mother sat back as if struck.

Amaranth knew when her mother crept into the hotel hallway at night and murmured on her cell phone that she had bred a new terror between Otto and her mother. What if Amaranth wouldn't get into college. How long would they have to be saddled with the burden of her. Under the spoken words of donations suggested, trustees summoned, plans set out, was the silent undercurrent, that fear of a five-foot skeleton; didn't they deserve a rest?

And so, when she and her mother returned to the house the next day in time for lunch, Amaranth shyly asked Otto what, exactly, a hedge fund *did*. And Otto answered in equally soft tones. And Amaranth asked the smartest questions she could about arbitrage, about compensation, about futures. When Amaranth bent her docile head to take a bite of salmon, she could sense the delighted glance the two others shared.

Problem solved, and so easily, too. Amaranth would finish the summer as Otto's intern.

She was put in the copy room and faxed, duplicated, fetched paper and coffee. Some touch of her story must have leaked among the others; she was treated gently and smiled upon. She would wake before dawn to ride her horse and, showered, in her black suit bought from the children's department, would eat a quick breakfast of croissant and espresso with her mother. Then the car would pull up, and she would watch the landscape and Otto would frown at his laptop or newspaper, and the driver would end at the revolving brass door.

It was so easy, this life. When she looked coldly, she could see that if she just let go, if she went along with what they wanted and no longer privately fought, it could all end happily. The family close and loving, a life beyond the house good and whole, the half-whisper she heard with every heartbeat going silent, then dying. She made herself remember the wet spill of her father's head on the pavement. She had to focus to keep it alive.

In August, she noticed the new topiarist at the house, a Belgian man in his mid-twenties who was so conflicted about his poor English he hardly spoke at all. He had powerful shoulders, a small hard stomach, a good jaw, eyes like blackberries. She'd seen him watching her when she rode the horse past the greenhouse in the morning, and what had been a vague and distant idea hove startling near. She looked at herself critically later in her jodhpurs, and saw a body that could be a boy's or a child's. Well, there was no knowing what men wanted; it'd be an advantage, she saw, for the tastes of some.

And so one day she slid off her horse and nodded at the man. He stood. She left the horse tied to a hedge and took the man behind the summer house, between the blue hydrangeas and the stone wall. He was compliant as a mannequin as she straddled him and spat into her hand and lowered herself down, bearing the pain. He touched her not at all.

Later, in the bathtub, there was a faint pink ribbon coming from her, something internal broken.

This too was a power.

She tested it. At work, she took into the closet a fat curly-headed college graduate, a boy whose brain danced balletically in numbers, who protested the whole time and in two strokes gasped into her. School began, a new one in the city where nobody knew of her illnesses. And though it was a girls' school, there was a boys' school just down the street. In the graveyard of the church between, a hidden corner of buttress and wall, her tiny hands on the boys' hot crotches, so eager they barely made it into the cold before spitting and shriveling. Her new violin teacher, a Juilliard student with a goiterous Adam's apple, who only let her near him if she played her scales faultlessly. A stranger in a coffee-shop bathroom, jamming her head against the tile wall again and again, her knees and palms pressed in purple grids for hours afterward.

The topiarist, who tried to warm her haunches, bared to the air, with his hands. He, who tried to kiss her and she ducked her cheek away. He, who, in the gravel outroom of the greenhouse where the topiaries overwintered like vast green goddesses, unpinned a heap of burlap sacks and revealed a sculptured colt, teeth bared, neck turned painfully to bite itself. It was her, she saw. He understood her, though they had never spoken more than a few words. She touched the colt's fine shoulders of bay laurel and had to turn and leave the gardener alone with his gift.

She tried her doctor, but he fended off her hands calmly and firmly, saying, You mustn't touch me like this. And though she didn't like his no, she liked the panic she'd sparked in his eyes. Every session, she kept trying.

It was he, she knew, who eventually told her mother about the new shape Amaranth's demon had taken, and it was her mother who left her fears gift-wrapped on Amaranth's bed. A box of a hundred condoms, a box of Plan-B pills, a book ludicrously titled *Embracing Your Sexuality: Teenage Edition*.

But when summer arrived again and Amaranth came downstairs in her business suit, with her wet hair, she found Otto had already been driven off, and that her mother would be taking her into the city. She understood, then, that Otto knew what she'd been doing and that he'd been avoiding being alone with her. She felt, first, a slow welling of grief. Then the grief died away, and she was woozy with victory.

∽⊘⌇

When she walked into the firm, it was clear that measures had been taken to keep her from the men. She had her own office, once a supply closet, next to the photocopying and shredding and faxing room. She was given a low-level number-crunching job, solitary and brain-killing, a job that a monkey could do.

This is what they thought she was, a monkey, the boss's kid, seventeen-but-looks-twelve, sick. Something wrong with her. Pitiful object, sexless or oversexed or something. Merry! they called for her when she went to refill her water bottle, fax this. Merry, be a peach and shred this stack, please, Merry, I need some more toner, Merry, could you make sure this gets to Japan in the next hour, please. And she bit her tongue, she smiled weakly, she did as they asked. And she took their files and faxes and photocopies into her office and pored over them. She copied, she secreted papers under her suit, she took them home.

In the topiarist's closet above a wine shop, a tower of Bankers Boxes was forming; a case was building itself. She hadn't known what she was looking for until she found it. This discrepancy. This careless note.

It was time, she decided. The path had finally come clear.

She took calcium tablets, multivitamins, fish oil, she ate full-fat Greek yogurt and egg whites. Her body, which she had kept so small for so long, woke. She grew two inches in a month; her bones ached in the night. She studied herself in her mirror, doing crunches and pushups and core exercises, running six miles at dawn. She grew breasts. A-cup, B-cup, enough to push together to make cleavage.

When she arrived at the topiarist's at night, he closed his eyes when he was with her, and sometimes he couldn't even begin. They spooned then, warmth against warmth, and when he fell asleep, she reluctantly stood and left.

On her lunch break, she bought revealing clothing, left a button unbuttoned here and there. Her hair grew long enough for a knot at the nape, her eye makeup grew complicated. She began to look like what she was, somewhere between a child and a woman.

One morning in August, she slid into the idling car before Otto and when he climbed in, he looked startled to find her there. I thought I'd get an early ride in, she said, beaming.

He put aside his newspaper and looked at her sternly. I have to do work, he said, and opened his laptop and ignored her.

She watched the landscape contentedly. Her presence, today, was enough.

∽☙⤳

Begin softly. Stay late; stay past the custodians vacuuming, dumping the wastepaper baskets; meet at the elevator, apologetic. Walk down to the car in silence. When his head is back and he's pretending to doze in the car, take the newspaper off his lap, brushing the fabric gently with your fingertips. When at breakfast your mother tells her husband she's excited to see him at lunch, show up uninvited to the restaurant and sit down at the table, submit to your mother's effusions of gladness, let your foot graze a trousered leg more times than could be accidental. Wake up early, steal a ride. Stay late, steal a ride. Paint your toenails in the seat opposite, lifting a knee, letting your skirt fold back, tiny pot red as blood between your fingers. Watch him look, look away. Watch him look again, longer now, quick and hungry. Watch the grass crisp brown in the summer heat. Repeat.

On Sunday, when your mother is at the masseuse, lie back in a green bikini at the time when he comes to swim laps in the pool. Watch the awkward crab-walk across the deck, the obvious avoidance. Laugh into your elbow. Start up the sauna. Pour water on the electric rocks. Take off the wet green bikini. Breathe in the cedar heat. Patience. Years and years, you have waited for this, you have set things into irreversible motion, you can see the gleaming end.

The dark will swing open to a door-sized light. A body will hesitate there. The door will close. The body will come nearer, out of the dark; a hand will touch your cheek.

∽☙⤳

Amaranth watched it multiply, from the town car's backseat, curtain closed, to the greenhouse on the gardener's day off, among the misted poinsettias and the grim, gray river, sluggish outside.

Amaranth's mother had her face lifted and it sat swollen in gauze; as she lay in a dark room, Amaranth stripped for Otto in his office, slowly, watching him watch her take off one sock, another, her bra. His hands shook. After, he gave her a bracelet, an enameled goldfish swallowing its own tail. Fifteen minutes later, Amaranth brought her mother a raspberry smoothie and felt Otto's hands still on her thighs. Her mother's eyes were bald baby mice among the bandages.

Amaranth was accepted early to the school of her choice, and they celebrated with champagne. It still hurt her mother to smile; she couldn't stop smiling.

In the Christmas picture they sent out for the first and last time ever, they looked as close to happy as they ever were. Her mother held Amaranth on one side, laughing, looking twenty years younger than she was. Otto was on Amaranth's other side, his arm around both women. Amaranth alone wasn't smiling, though her face was alight with something that was difficult to look at directly.

∽❧∼

In February, Amaranth came into her stepfather's study and locked the door. Her mother was in the exercise room with the Pilates instructor.

Hey, he said and pushed his work to the side of the desk, sat back, expectant.

She inserted herself between his legs, and put a disc in his laptop.

What's this? he said. His hand stilled where he had put it on her thigh.

A gift, she said lightly. To me.

Playing, now, on his computer: the unspeakable. To film it, Amaranth had used the teddy bear her mother had once used to spy on Rosalie. They were in Amaranth's bedroom, still childish with its wallpaper full of prancing horses. It took a moment to see Amaranth tiny under Otto's big body on the bed. She was drawn up in a ball to appear even smaller. He held her wrists above her head with one hand, held her throat with the other. By her grimace of pain, one would never have guessed that she had begged him to do this moments before.

No, he said. What?

She pulled a piece of paper to her and wrote a figure, then the number of a Swiss bank account.

This is insane, he said. I refuse.

You have twenty-four hours, she said. Or I go to my mother.

No, he said.

Yes, she said.

He took off his glasses and rubbed his fleshy face. She walked out. When she closed the door, she sank against it, unable to breathe. He was called suddenly to the office for urgent business and stayed in the city. In the morning, she found the money where she knew it would be.

⟡

Otto was in Europe a lot in the spring for business, vaguely. Her mother took the opportunity to liposuction her thighs and sides. She minced around in bandages. Amaranth fetched her broth and toast, brushed her dark hair out on the pillow, pulled the gray with tweezers.

There was a part of Amaranth that wanted to withhold the final piece. To believe that what she had done already was enough. The summer was long and gentle, her mother and she going to the beach together, going to movies, coming to a quiet accord. Banana bread baking in the morning. Coddled eggs on beds of spinach at night.

But the week before she went off to college, Amaranth woke in a panic. Something had called to her, and she listened for a long time, but heard nothing except her nerves jangling, some frogs outside, an owl. She remembered the bell in the winter wind so many years ago, its frantic ringing. She listened, but heard no bell. Maybe only the echo of its absence.

She had been taking notes all along. She knew the right zealot to approach. She had watched him on television, had seen the speeches he gave. He was sleek in his suit, with a shiny forehead, a weak chin. A small man, of course. They always are.

She made contact in the morning, and he returned her call immediately. She let herself into the topiarist's while he was at work and drove the Bankers Boxes of papers into the city. The handover was simple and neat. The zealot looked at her without blinking, sweating through his charcoal suit.

During finals week of her first semester at college, she looked up from her calculus textbook to see Otto on the television. He was being escorted by grim dark men, his hands were behind his back, his pasty face was startled, blinking behind his glasses. He focused on the camera and she thought, for a second, that he was looking through the screen at her, into her black little heart. But she had been careful. He would never know that she had been the architect of this ruin. Impossible: she was Merry, sick and weak. She watched as his head was pushed down into a car and he was driven off.

She wasn't sure what she was tasting in her mouth. It was either flesh or ashes.

For a long while, at least an hour, she let her cell phone ring and go to voicemail, ring and go to voicemail. She stood in a hot shower, letting it sear her clean. Only when she was weak from the heat did she put her hair in a towel and a robe on her body and crawl into bed and call her mother back. At first, her mother could find no words to describe what had happened. For a long time she only sobbed. And when she began to speak, Amaranth heard the faltering beginnings of her mother's understanding that her life was falling apart around her, block by block, the whole castle crumbling, and it was all Amaranth could do not to laugh.

ABOUT THE EDITORS

MOLLY LLEWELLYN IS A twenty-something queer, disabled book blogger from the UK. She is half of the editing team for *Peach Pit* coming Fall 2023 from Dzanc, which is her first big editing role. She's a big fan of 'weird women' lit and anything that is the colour green. She lives in the UK.

KRISTEL BUCKLEY IS AN editor, publicist and former publisher from the Big Smoke. She is more than happy to talk your ear off about the unfaithful representation of women in history, and her passion is a more equitable, inclusive future for all stories from all voices. She lives in the UK.

ABOUT THE CONTRIBUTORS

ALICE ASH IS THE author of the short story collection *Paradise Block*, which won The Edge Hill Short Story Readers' Prize in 2021. She was longlisted for the Galley Beggar Short Story Prize in 2019, and other writing has been featured in *Granta, Refinery29, 3:AM, Hotel, Extra Teeth Magazine, the TLS*, and *Mslexia*, amongst many others. Interests include motherhood, women's horror writing, domesticity, magical realism, and metamorphosis. Alice's second book, a novel, will be published by Serpent's Tail in 2024. Alice teaches at the University of Westminster and Goldsmiths University, and she is an editor with The Literary Consultancy. She lives in the UK.

ALICIA ELLIOTT IS A Mohawk writer and editor living in Ontario. She has written for *The Globe and Mail, CBC, Hazlitt* and many others. She's had numerous essays nominated for National Magazine Awards, winning Gold in 2017 and an honourable mention in 2020. Her short fiction was selected for *Best American Short Stories* 2018 (by Roxane Gay), *Best Canadian Stories* 2018, and *Journey Prize Stories* 30. Alicia was chosen by Tanya Talaga as the 2018 recipient of the RBC Taylor Emerging Writer Award. Her first book, *A Mind Spread Out On The Ground*, was a national bestseller in Canada. It was also nominated for the Hilary Weston Writers' Trust Prize for Nonfiction, and won the Forest of Reading Evergreen Award.

A LISON RUMFITT IS A writer and semi-professional trans woman. *Tell Me I'm Worthless*, her debut novel, was published in 2021 by Cipher Press in the UK and in 2023 by Tor Nightfire in the US. Her second novel, *Brainwyrms*, is coming October 2023. She lives in the UK.

A LIYA WHITELEY'S NOVELS AND novellas have been shortlisted for multiple awards including the Arthur C Clarke award and a Shirley Jackson award. Her short fiction has appeared in *Interzone, Beneath Ceaseless Skies, F&SF, Black Static, Strange Horizons, The Dark, McSweeney's Internet Tendency* and *The Guardian*, as well as in anthologies such as Unsung Stories' *2084* and Lonely Planet's *Better than Fiction*. She writes in many genres, she takes a lot of long walks during which she thinks up strange things, and she bakes a mean choc chip vanilla cookie. She lives in the UK.

A MANDA LEDUC IS THE author of the novel *The Centaur's Wife* and the non-fiction book *Disfigured: On Fairy Tales, Disability, and Making Space*, which was shortlisted for the 2020 Governor General's Award in Nonfiction (Canada) and longlisted for the 2020 Barbellion Prize (UK). She is also the author of an earlier novel, *The Miracles of Ordinary Men*. She has cerebral palsy and lives in Hamilton, Ontario, where she serves as the Communications Coordinator for the Festival of Literary Diversity (FOLD), Canada's first festival for diverse authors and stories.

C HANA PORTER IS A novelist, playwright, teacher, MacDowell fellow, and cofounder of The Octavia Project, a STEM and writing program for girls and trans and nonbinary youth that uses speculative fiction to envision greater possibilities for our world. Her debut novel *The Seep* was an ABA Indie Next Pick, Open Letters Best Science Fiction & Fantasy Book of 2020, a 2021 Lambda Literary Award Finalist, and a Times (UK) Best Sci-fi Book of 2021. As a playwright, her work has been produced and developed at New Georges, Playwrights Horizons, Cherry Lane, Dixon Place, Target Margin, and many more. Her second novel *The Thick and The Lean* is out from Saga/Simon & Schuster spring 2023. Chana is currently adapting Ursula K. Le Guin's *The Dispossessed* into an opera with the composer Ted Hearne. She lives in Los Angeles. Pronouns: she/they

CHANTAL V. JOHNSON IS a lawyer and writer. Her debut novel, *Post-Traumatic*, was long-listed for the Center for Fiction First Novel Prize. A graduate of Stanford Law School and a former Center for Fiction Emerging Writers Fellow, she lives in New York.

CHAYA BHUVANESWAR IS A practicing physician, writer and PEN /American Robert W. Bingham Debut Fiction award finalist for her story collection *White Dancing Elephants: Stories*, which was also selected as a Kirkus Reviews Best Debut Fiction and Best Short Story Collection and appeared on "best of" lists for *Harper's Bazaar, Elle, Vogue India*, and *Entertainment Weekly*. Her work has appeared in *The New York Times, Salon, Narrative Magazine, Tin House, Electric Literature, Kenyon Review, Masters Review, The Millions, Joyland, Michigan Quarterly Review, The Awl*, and elsewhere. She has received fellowships from MacDowell, Community of Writers and Sewanee Writers Workshop. She lives in Massachusetts.

DEESHA PHILYAW'S DEBUT SHORT story collection, *The Secret Lives of Church Ladies*, won the 2021 PEN/Faulkner Award for Fiction, the 2020/2021 Story Prize, and the 2020 LA Times Book Prize: The Art Seidenbaum Award for First Fiction and was a finalist for the 2020 National Book Award for Fiction. *The Secret Lives of Church Ladies* focuses on Black women, sex, and the Black church, and is being adapted for television by HBO Max with Tessa Thompson executive producing. Deesha is also a Kimbilio Fiction Fellow and was the 2022-2023 John and Renee Grisham Writer-in-Residence at the University of Mississippi. Deesha lives in California.

K-MING CHANG IS A Kundiman fellow, a Lambda Literary Award finalist, and a National Book Foundation 5 Under 35 honoree. She is the author of the *New York Times Book Review* Editors' Choice books *Bestiary* and *Gods of Want* (One World/Random House), and two forthcoming books, a novel titled *Organ Meats* (One World) and a novella titled *Cecilia* (Coffee House Press). She lives in California.

L AUREN GROFF IS THE author of six books of fiction, the most recent the novel *Matrix* (September 2021). Her work has won The Story Prize, the ABA Indies' Choice Award, and France's Grand Prix de l'Héroïne, was a three time finalist for the National Book Award for Fiction and twice for the Kirkus Prize, and was shortlisted for the National Book Critics Circle Prize, the Southern Book Prize, and the Los Angeles Times Prize. She has received fellowships from the Guggenheim Foundation and the Radcliffe Institute for Advanced Study, and was named one of Granta's Best of Young American Novelists. Her work has been translated into over thirty languages. She lives in Florida.

M AISY CARD IS THE author of the novel *These Ghosts are Family*, which won an American Book Award, the 2021 OCM Bocas Prize in Fiction and was a finalist for the PEN/Hemingway Award for Debut Novel, The Center for Fiction First Novel Prize, and the LA Times Art Seidenbaum Award. Her writing has appeared in *The Paris Review Daily, AGNI, The New York Times, Guernica*, and other publications. She lives in New Jersey.

Megan Giddings is an assistant professor at the University of Minnesota. Her first novel, *Lakewood*, was a finalist for two NAACP Image Awards and an LA Times Book Prize. Her second novel, *The Women Could Fly*, was a *New York Times* Editor's Choice, one of *Washington Post*'s Best Science Fiction and Fantasy Novels of 2022, and one of *Vulture*'s 10 Best Fantasy Novels of 2022. Megan's work has been supported by Hedgebrook and The Barbara Deming Foundation. More about her can be found at www.megangiddings.com

Sarah Rose Etter is the author of *The Book of X*, winner of a Shirley Jackson Award, and the novel *Ripe* (Scribner, July 2023). Her work has appeared in *TIME, Bomb, The Cut, Vice, Oxford American*, and more. You can find out more at www.sarahroseetter.com. She lives in California.

Vanessa Chan was born and raised in Malaysia. *The Storm We Made*, her first novel, will be published in 2024 in twenty languages and territories, including with Marysue Rucci Books/Simon & Schuster (US) and Hodder & Stoughton (UK). Her story collection, *The Ugliest Babies in the World*, is also forthcoming. Her other writing has been published in *Electric Lit, Kenyon Review, Ecotone*, and more. She lives in the U.S.

Yah Yah Scholfield is a horror artiste, Brooklyn born and Atlanta raised. Their work can be found in *Fiyah Lit* magazine, and a handful of other magazines and anthologies. They published their debut novel *On Sundays, She Picked Flowers* in 2022, and their short story collection *Just a Little Snack* is forthcoming November 2023 from Nyx Publishing. When Yah Yah is not crafting horrors, they're working as a professional stay-at-home daughter and wrangler of their two cats, Sophie and Chihiro. They live in the US.

ACKNOWLEDGMENTS

WITH THANKS FIRST AND FOREMOST to the sixteen contributing authors, without whom this anthology would not be what it is—it's been an absolute honour and joy getting to work alongside some of today's finest writers. Thank you to our brilliant literary agent, Serene Hakim, who has been the most patient, supportive, and understanding guide since day one. Thankyou to our editor at Dzanc, Michelle Dotter for your passion and belief in our collection and giving it the most perfect home (indie presses forever!!) Thank you to the besties Zara and Saff for being my sounding board and keeping me sane during this whole process and my family for their constant support. And if you've got this far, thank you to you the reader for taking time to read these nasty little stories, it means the world. ~ Molly Llewellyn

ECHOING WHAT MOLLY HAS SAID, I cannot thank these sixteen authors more; their characters will forever live in a space inside my head, and I am going to try my best not to take their advice on how to approach things! These authors have been an absolute joy, and I feel very lucky to have worked with them to create this book. Thank you to Serene and Michelle for making this come true, the effort and dedication you've both given to this book is just as important as the words themselves. More personally, thank you to Lucy Rose, Luella Williamson, and Toph Turner for teaching me every day to be better, and of course to my mother, whose layers I am still discovering. Finally, to you the reader, sometimes we just need to read a story like these to stop us from making a story like these! ~ Kristel Buckley